"Don't want to get too comfortable here?"

Wyatt's scent—all warm, sexy man—sent another thrill thrumming through her. She rose, clothing in hand. Determined to be practical, even if he wouldn't be. "More like I don't want to overstep my bounds. Become even more intrusive to your living space than the twins and I already are."

"Hey." He caught her arm and reeled her back into his side. "Are you unhappy here?"

"No. It's just…" She tried to ignore the way his gaze scanned the V of her robe. "You and I have made a lot of changes really quickly."

"Because we had to," he countered, all implacable male. "What I want to know is why you're suddenly running so hot and cold again."

Exasperated, Adelaide ran both her hands through her hair. "I'm unnerved because we're doing what we always do! Getting way, way ahead of ourselves!"

Wyatt gathered her in his arms. "No," he countered gruffly, smoothing the hair from her face. "We're catching up."

The Texas
Valentine Twins

CATHY GILLEN
THACKER

MILLS & BOON

First Published in Great Britain 2017
By Mills & Boon, an imprint of HarperCollins*Publishers*
1 London Bridge Street, London, SE1 9GF

Large Print edition 2017

© 2017 Cathy Gillen Thacker

ISBN: 978-0-263-07179-5

Printed and bound in Great Britain
by CPI Antony Rowe, Chippenham, Wiltshire

Cathy Gillen Thacker is married and a mother of three. She and her husband spent eighteen years in Texas and now reside in North Carolina. Her mysteries, romantic comedies and heartwarming family stories have made numerous appearances on bestseller lists, but her best reward, she says, is knowing one of her books made someone's day a little brighter. A popular Mills & Boon author for many years, she loves telling passionate stories with happy endings and thinks nothing beats a good romance and a hot cup of tea! You can visit Cathy's website, www.cathygillenthacker.com, for more information on her upcoming and previously published books, recipes and a list of her favorite things.

Chapter One

"When were you going to tell me?" Wyatt Lock-hart demanded. He was obviously furious.

Adelaide Smythe looked at the ruggedly hand-some rancher standing on the front stoop of her Laramie, Texas, cottage and tried not to react. An impossible task, given the way her heart sped up and her knees went all wobbly any time he was within sight.

Purposefully ignoring the intent look in his way-too-mesmerizing smoky blue eyes, she picked up both duffel bags of baby clothes, blankets and burp cloths and carried them to her waiting SUV.

Aware he was still waiting for an answer, she stated coolly over her shoulder, "I wasn't."

Wyatt moved so she had no choice but to look up at him.

He looked good, but then he always looked good in the way of strong, tall and sexy. Radiating an impressive amount of testosterone and kick-butt attitude, he stood, brawny arms folded in front of him, legs braced apart. Back against the rear corner of her vehicle.

His gaze drifted over her, as if he were appraising one of the impeccably trained cutting horses that he bred and sold on his ranch. "You didn't think I would find out?"

Adelaide tensed. Of course she had known.

She shrugged, her carelessness in direct counterpoint to his concern, and slid the duffels into the cargo area next to the boxes of diapers and formula.

Finished, she lifted her chin defiantly and

looked into the piercing gaze that always saw way more than she would have preferred. "I knew your mother might mention it, eventually." Just as she had intuited that the most cynical of the Lockhart sons would be more than just a little unhappy when he heard about the arrangements.

Wyatt stepped back as if to ward off a punch. "My mom knows?"

It was her ranch. Of course Lucille Lockhart knew Adelaide and the twins were moving temporarily into the Circle H bunkhouse the following week!

Wondering how Wyatt imagined she could manage this without the matriarch's explicit permission, Adelaide favored him with a deadpan expression. "It was Lucille's idea, obviously." As was the notion that Adelaide start bringing over the things she was going to need now, instead of waiting and trying to do it and transport her six-week-old twins all at one time.

Again, Wyatt shook his head as if that would clear it. His sensual lips compressed into a thin, hard line. "I know the two of you have always been close."

An understatement, Adelaide thought. In many ways Lucille Lockhart had been the loving maternal force her life lacked. Even before her father had betrayed everyone they knew and taken off with a gold-digging floozy. "Yes. We have."

Wyatt took off his hat and shoved his fingers through the thick, straight layers of his wheat-colored hair. Frowning, he settled his Stetson square on his head and met her gaze head-on. "I still find it hard to believe my mother talked you into this travesty."

Adelaide didn't see what was so difficult to understand. If Wyatt had a single compassionate bone in his body, he would have extended a helping hand, too. If for no other reason than their two families had once been very close. "Lucille knows how I've been struggling to manage in the six and a half weeks since my children were born. She thought some assistance…" Some help feeding and diapering and rocking…

His brow lifted. He cut in sharply, all harsh male judgment once again. "Financial, I suppose?"

A mixture of embarrassment and humiliation filled Adelaide with heat. She'd never imagined needing a helping hand. But since she suddenly did…she would accept it on behalf of her twins

Adelaide marched back to the porch, tension shimmering through her frame. Aware only a small part of any of this was her doing, she picked up the large monogrammed designer suitcase that held her own clothing. The one that, unfortunately, had been given to her as a high school graduation gift. And had accompanied her on another, fortuitously ill-begotten, trip.

The way Wyatt was eyeing it said he remembered, too.

Refusing to think about what he might be recalling about their hopelessly romantic—and ill-fated—adventure, she continued, "If you consider being guests at her ranch for a couple months so I won't have to pay rent on top of my mortgage and new construction loan…"

He definitely did.

She squared her shoulders and admitted reluctantly, "Then yes, I do need some financial help, and in many other ways, as well. Things have been hard for me, since my father left Texas…"

Seeing how she was struggling under the weight of her bag, Wyatt reached over and took it from her. In two quick strides he carried it to the cargo area and set it next to the two smaller duffels. "Don't you mean since he embezzled funds from my family's charitable foundation and then fled the country?"

Her shame over that fact only increased as time passed. Adelaide tossed in a mesh bag of soft infant toys. Figuring she had done enough packing for now, she slammed the lid on the cargo hold. "I've apologized every way I know how for that." A fact that Wyatt very well knew, gosh darn it.

She stomped closer, determined to have this

out once and for all, so they'd never have to discuss it again. "Everyone else in your family has forgiven me," she reminded him.

He remained where he was. Which was…too close. Far too close. He leaned down, inundating her with the scent of sun-warmed leather and soap. "So they're more foolhardy than I am," he said.

Adelaide glared at him. She knew Wyatt was still angry with her. And that his anger was based on a lot more than the sins of her father. The thing was, she was grief stricken over their failed romance, too. The knowledge that their dreams were never going to come true.

Ignoring the heat and strength radiating from his tall body, Adelaide stepped around him and headed wearily for the porch. Unable to help the defeated slump of her slender shoulders, she asked, "When are you going to let our last mistake go?"

He caught up with her and joined her on the small porch. Hooking his thumbs through the loops on either side of his belt, he murmured silkily, "I never said making love with you bothered me."

It had sure as heck bothered her! To the point she barely slept a night without reliving that reckless misstep in her dreams. Refusing to admit how many mornings she had awakened hugging her pillow as if it were the answer to her every wish and desire, Adelaide challenged him with a smile.

"Then that makes two of us," she drawled, refusing to admit how small his six-foot-three frame made the four-by-four-foot square beneath the portico feel.

Wyatt paused. His gaze roamed her postpregnancy frame, dwelling on the voluptuousness of her curves. "Enough to go again?" he taunted softly.

So that was it, she realized with a mixture of excitement and resentment. He still desired her every bit as much as she yearned for him. Fortunately for both of them, she was sensible enough not to repeat their error. Even if her obstetrician had given her the go ahead at her last checkup.

Adelaide stiffened. "Not if we were the last two people on earth," she vowed.

THE LOOK IN Adelaide's eyes had Wyatt believing her.

The knowledge of what she had done—or more precisely *hadn't* done—convinced him otherwise.

Wishing he no longer found her thick mane of chocolate-brown hair and wide-set sable eyes so alluring, he stepped closer still. Deliberately invading her personal space, he let his gaze drift over the elegant features of her face, lingering on her slightly upturned nose, the prominent cheekbones and lushness of her lips.

Body hardening, he demanded, "Then why did you concoct such a harebrained plan with my mother?" If that was indeed the case. He still found it hard to believe that his mother had played matchmaker.

Adelaide blinked at him and furrowed her brow. "Why do you care where the twins and I live while the addition is being built on my home?"

Her innocence was real enough to be believed...had he not been the recipient of her heart-rending, soul-crushing antics. He knew, better than anyone, what she was like deep down. Reeling him in, and promising one thing, then actually delivering on another...

Luckily, his broken heart had mended.

"Even if it is technically on your mother's property," Adelaide continued irritably.

It was his turn to do a double take. He studied the riotous blush of pink on her pretty face. "You think I'm ticked off about you and your kids moving into the bunkhouse on the Circle H?"

Adelaide lounged against the opposite post. She folded her arms in front of her, the action plumping her newly voluptuous breasts even more. She regarded him with contempt. "Aren't you?"

He wouldn't lie. "I think it's a bad idea." One of the worst, actually.

Her lower lip thrust out in the way that always made him want to haul her into his arms and kiss her. "Why?"

He remained on his side of the small covered porch with effort. Getting emotionally entangled with this woman again would not serve either of them. "I don't want to see my mother taken advantage of by your family again." The first time had been bad enough.

Adelaide sent him a withering glare. "I'm not my father."

She was right about that. In some respects, she was worse. Paul Smythe's actions had been aimed at the bank account. Adelaide's targeted… the heart.

He pulled a folded envelope from a back pocket of his jeans. Still holding her turbulent gaze, he handed it over. "I would have believed that if I hadn't seen this," he told her gruffly.

Adelaide stared at the logo on the outside of

the folded business letter, announcing the information was from the Texas Metro Detective Agency. Farther down, it was addressed to Wyatt Lockhart, regarding background information on Adelaide Smythe.

The color drained from her face. He watched her shiver, although the temperature was mild for the last day of January. She stared up at him in disbelief. "You actually had me investigated?"

She'd given him no choice. "The minute I heard my mother had invited you-all to stay at her place indefinitely. And you made her Jenny and Jake's godmother and 'honorary grandmother.'"

Adelaide looked like she wanted to kick him in the shin. "You really are unbelievable," she sputtered.

Refusing to allow her indignation to sway him from the facts, he countered harshly, "Don't you want to know what I found out?"

Recovering, she handed him the report, said with cool disdain, "Well, obviously you're dying to tell me, so far be it from me to stop you."

If she wanted to play dumb, he could draw it out mercilessly, too. "Remember Vegas?" The most wildly romantic and absolutely soul-crushing time of their teenage courtship?

Her spine turned as stiff and unyielding as her mood. "I'd rather not."

He agreed with her there. Their hasty elopement hadn't turned out the way he'd envisioned. Her, either, judging from the blotchy red and white hue of her skin.

"It wasn't just the wedding night you had trouble following through on," he told her sarcastically, still not sure this wasn't some kind of ruse cooked up by her, long ago, left to wreak havoc on him now. Seeing he had her complete attention, he continued, "You had a little difficulty with the paperwork, too."

For a moment, she seemed not to even breathe. She regarded him warily. "What are you talking about?" she bit out finally.

His worst nightmare come true, obviously. "We're still married."

Chapter Two

A whisper of fear threaded through Adelaide. What Wyatt was suggesting was even worse than the thought that he might have somehow discovered the disturbing messages she'd been getting through her social media accounts. Messages that were also tied to her past, although in a different venue.

This was dangerous territory. "Stop clowning around."

Scowling, he stood with his hands on his hips. "Do I look like I'm joking?"

No, he most certainly did not. A fact that unsettled her even more than the person *pretending* to be her MIA father. "Look, I don't know who you talked to, Wyatt, but I signed everything and paid the lawyer the wedding chapel recommended before I left Nevada."

His jaw took on a don't-mess-with-me tilt. He stepped close enough she could almost touch the rough stubble lining his impossibly masculine jaw. "Then why isn't there any record of the dissolution of our marriage?" he demanded gruffly.

Deciding being close enough to kiss was a terrible idea, Adelaide backed up. "I don't know. Maybe you hired an incompetent private investigator."

"And maybe the annulment was never filed," Wyatt bit out. "Which is why I've asked Gannon Montgomery to meet us here in five minutes."

The former Fort Worth attorney, now married and living in Laramie, had handled lots of clients with family money, fame and fortune, including a case involving the former Dallas quarter-back's son.

Adelaide should have known that her ex would revert to a legal solution to a very personal problem that, had they both been reasonable, would not have required any outside intervention.

"Fine," she huffed, ready to call in her own ace attorney. She whipped out her cell phone. "You want lawyers involved? I'm calling mine, too."

Luckily, it was the very end of the work day, and Claire McCabe was still in her office. She agreed to come right over. So by the time Adelaide had brewed a pot of coffee, Claire McCabe and Gannon Montgomery had both arrived.

Big and handsome, Gannon was a few years older than she and Wyatt. Claire was in her mid-fifties. She had two adopted children, and was the go-to attorney in the area for families who had children in extraordinary ways. Adelaide had always found Claire sympathetic and kind, and today, to her relief, she seemed to have extra helpings of both ready to dish out.

"So where are the twins?" Claire asked warmly.

"Upstairs, sleeping." Adelaide glanced at her watch. "Hopefully for at least another half an hour."

"Then let's get to it, shall we?" Claire suggested.

Gannon sat at the dining table next to Wyatt. Claire sat next to Adelaide. While she poured coffee, Gannon and Claire perused the documents, then did quick searches on their laptops for any verification of an annulment. "I'm not finding any," Claire said. "Under either of their names."

"Nor am I," Gannon added. "Although their marriage comes up right away, on Valentine's Day, almost ten years ago."

"So that means the detective agency is right," Wyatt presumed, big hands gripping the mug in front of him. "Adelaide and I are still legally married?"

He looked about as happy as Adelaide felt.

Claire and Gannon nodded.

Adelaide did her best to quell her racing pulse. Even bad situations had solutions. "What will it take to get an annulment?" she asked casually.

More typing on the computers followed as both attorneys researched Nevada law.

"Were you underage?" Gannon asked.

Adelaide admitted reluctantly, "We were both eighteen. No parental permission was required."

"Incapacitated in some way?" Claire queried. "Mentally, emotionally? Either of you intoxicated or high?"

Wyatt and Adelaide shook their heads. "We knew what we were doing," he said.

In that sense, maybe, Adelaide thought, recalling how immature they had been. They hadn't had any idea what it really meant to be *married*. Since both of them had remained single, they probably still didn't know.

Gannon exhaled roughly. "Then you're going to have to claim fraud."

"I'm not doing that," Adelaide cut in. Not with her family's reputation.

"Well, don't look at *me*. I'm not the one who changed my mind and backed out," Wyatt said.

Claire lifted a hand and intervened gently. "Why don't you tell us what happened?"

Adelaide flushed. Reluctant to discuss how foolishly romantic she had been, when they had set out for Vegas, after both had fought with their parents about the too-serious nature of their relationship. How determined they were to do something to show everyone, only to find out how scary it was to truly be in over their heads.

Adelaide drew a deep breath. "We eloped without thinking everything through."

Wyatt sat back in his chair, the implacable look she hated in his smoky blue eyes. "What she's trying to say is that she got cold feet."

"Came to my senses," Adelaide corrected him archly, irritated to find he still hadn't a compassionate bone in him. When he merely lifted a brow, she continued emotionally, "You did wild and reckless things all the time, growing up, Wyatt. I didn't."

He scoffed, hurt flashing across his handsome face. "Well, we sure found that out the hard way, didn't we?"

She knew she had disappointed him. She had disappointed herself. Though for entirely different reasons. Adelaide turned to their attorneys, explaining, "I was fine all through dinner, but when it came time to check into the hotel and consummate our union, I…" Choking up, Adelaide found herself unable to go on.

All eyes turned to Wyatt, who recounted dryly, "She panicked. Said she loved me, she just didn't want to be married to me, not yet." Accusation—and resentment—rang in his low tone.

Adelaide forced herself to ignore it, lest she too become caught up in an out-of-control emotional maelstrom. "I wanted to go home to Texas, finish our senior year of high school. And I wanted everything we had done, undone, without our families or anyone else finding out."

Wyatt, bless his heart, had agreed to let her have her way.

Unlike now.

Exhaling, he continued, "We went back to the wedding chapel and asked the justice of the peace who married us if he could pretend we had never been there. He refused. But he gave us the name of someone who could help us."

Adelaide remembered the relief she had felt. "So we went to the attorney's office the next day and asked him to file an annulment."

"I had a rodeo to compete in that evening, in Tahoe, so I signed what the attorney told me to sign and took off, leaving Adelaide behind to wrap things up."

"Which I did," Adelaide said hotly.

Wyatt lifted a brow. "You have a canceled check to prove it?"

His attitude was as contentious as his low,

clipped tone, but she refused to take the bait. "No. I paid his fee in cash."

Wyatt rocked back in his chair, ran the flat of his palm beneath his jaw. Finally, he shook his head and said, "Brilliant move."

Resisting the urge to leap across the table and take him by the collar, Adelaide folded her arms in front of her. "I was trying not to leave more of a paper trail than we already had."

Wyatt narrowed his gaze at her in mute superiority. "Learned from the best, there, didn't you?" he mocked.

Adelaide sucked in a startled breath. "*Do not* compare me with my father!" she snapped, her temper getting the better of her, despite her desire to appear cool, calm and collected. "If not for me, and all the forensic accounting work I did, people still might not know where all the money from the Lockhart Foundation went!"

An angry silence ticked out between them. Broken only by his taut reminder, "If not for *your father*, the foundation money might still all be there. My mother would not have been put through hell the last year."

Their gazes locked in an emotional battle of wills that had been years in the making. Refusing to give him a pass, even if he had been hurt and humiliated, too, she sent him a mildly rebuking look, even as the temperature between them rose to an unbearable degree. "Your mother knows I had nothing to do with any of that. So does the rest of your family." Ignoring the perspiration gathering between her breasts, she paused to let her words sink in. Dropped her voice another compelling notch. "Why can't you accept that, too?"

THE HELL OF it was, Wyatt secretly wished he could believe Adelaide Smythe was as innocent as everyone else did. He'd started to come close. And then *this* had happened.

He had seen Adelaide taking advantage of his mother's kindness and generosity, decided to investigate, just to reassure himself, and found even more corruption.

Claire and Gannon exchanged lawyerly looks. "Let's all calm down, shall we?" Gannon said.

Claire nodded. "Nothing will be gained from fighting."

Adelaide pushed her fingers through the dark strands of her hair. It spilled over her shoulders in sexy disarray. "You're right. Let's just focus on getting the annulment, which should be easy—" she paused to glare at Wyatt "—since we never consummated the marriage."

Once again, she was a little shady on the details. "Not then," Wyatt pointed out.

Adelaide paled, as if suddenly realizing what he already had.

Claire's brow furrowed. "You've been together intimately in the ten years since?"

Wyatt nodded, as another memory that had been hopelessly sexy and romantic took on a nefarious quality. "Last spring. After a destination wedding we both attended in Aspen."

A flush started in her chest and moved up her neck into her face. In a low, quavering voice,

Adelaide admitted, "We have a penchant for making terrible mistakes whenever we're alone together. But since we didn't know we were married at the time, that can't count as consummating the marriage." She gulped. "Can it?"

Stepping in, Gannon stated, "Actually, whether or not you slept together really doesn't affect the marriage's legality in the state of Texas. Hasn't for some time."

Wyatt and Adelaide both blinked in surprise.

"Emotionally, it might have ramifications," Claire interjected.

No kidding, Wyatt thought. Their one and only night together had sure left him feeling as if he had been rocketed to the moon, his every wish come true, and then…as soon as Adelaide had come to her senses…sucker punched in the gut by her. Again.

"Unless, of course, one of you is impotent and concealed it, which is clearly not the case," Gannon continued.

No kidding, Wyatt thought, remembering the

sparks that had been generated during his and Adelaide's one and only night together.

"You're saying we can't get an annulment?" Adelaide asked.

"Too much time has elapsed—nearly ten years—for you to request one from the court," Gannon said.

Claire soothed, "You can, however, get a divorce."

Wyatt knew what Adelaide was thinking. An annulment was a mistake, quickly remedied. A divorce meant being part of a marriage that had failed. That didn't sit well with her. He hated failing at anything, too.

"But we went to a lawyer at the time!" Adelaide protested.

Claire looked up from her computer. "Who, according to public record, has apparently not been a practicing member of the Nevada bar for nearly a decade."

Wyatt nodded. "The private detective agency said Mr. Randowsky had quit his practice and left the state shortly after we saw him. His practice dissolved accordingly."

Adelaide looked both shocked and crestfallen. "So there's no record of us ever being in his office? No real proof we ever tried to get an annulment?"

"None," Wyatt confirmed irritably. He had already been down that avenue with the private investigators. "I couldn't even locate anyone who worked in his office at the time."

Adelaide buried her head in her hands. "Which means that getting Mr. Randowsky or his former staff to testify on our behalf is a lost cause."

"Plus, there are children involved now," Claire pointed out.

Adelaide sat up abruptly, her pretty face a mask of maternal ferocity. *"My children,"* she stated tightly. "I went to a fertility clinic and was artificially inseminated two weeks before I saw Wyatt in Aspen."

Gannon looked at Wyatt. "You knew about this when you were together?"

Even as Wyatt shook his head, he knew it wouldn't have made any difference if he had. When he had seen her again that night, so happy and glowing and carefree, he had wanted her. She had wanted him, too. Recklessly. Wantonly.

And the rest was history.

"Adelaide didn't tell me she was starting a family until after I slept with her in Aspen." *"Nice as this was, and it was nice, nothing else can happen, Wyatt. I've got other plans…"*

She tossed her mane of glossy dark hair and gave him a defensive look. "It was a one-night stand, Wyatt. A kind of whimsical 'what if' for both of us ten years too late. I didn't think my pregnancy was relevant."

He hated her habit of downplaying what they had once meant to each other. Even if she hadn't had the guts to follow through. He looked her up and down, refusing to let her pretend any longer. "Oh, it was as relevant as the protection I wore."

Adelaide's mouth opened in a round O of surprise. "Wyatt!"

"Don't mind us," Gannon said dryly. "We're lawyers."

Claire added, "We've heard it all."

"Anyway," Wyatt stated, "I know what you're thinking." What he'd thought before reality and statistical probability crept in, given the fact that she'd already been inseminated and he'd worn a condom *every* time. "But the twins are not mine."

And he was glad of that. Wasn't he? Given the fact he still felt he couldn't quite trust her?

Adelaide's slender shoulders slumped slightly. "Thank heavens for small miracles!" she muttered with a beleaguered sigh.

She turned her glance away, but not before he saw the look of defeat in her eyes.

Wyatt felt a pang of remorse. So, the situation had ended up hurting her, too—despite her initial declarations to the contrary. Maybe he should try to go a little easier on her.

Certainly, they had enough strife ahead of them…

Oblivious to the ambivalence within him, Claire went back to taking notes. "So this… Adelaide's decision to have children via artificial insemination and sperm bank…is why you parted acrimoniously. Again."

Wyatt only wished it had been that simple. "I wouldn't have cared about that," he said honestly, ignoring Adelaide's embarrassment and looking her square in the eye.

Adelaide returned his level look. "Over time, you might have." She glanced at the baby monitor, as if hoping it would radiate young voices. It was silent. She cleared her throat, turned to regard their lawyers. "In any case, the insemination at the clinic took place before Wyatt and I ever saw each other again and were…reckless."

Reckless was one way to describe it, Wyatt mused. There was also passionate. Tender. Mind-blowing…

"And I was already sure I was pregnant…from the way I was feeling…"

Which was why, Wyatt thought, she'd been so

happy. In retrospect, he could see that it'd had little to do with seeing him again.

And for reasons he couldn't explain, and didn't want to examine, that stung, too.

More lawyerly looks were exchanged between the two attorneys.

Clearly, Wyatt noted, there was another problem.

Claire's brow furrowed. "Is the donor's name on the birth certificate?"

Adelaide shook her head. "No. Just mine. But I know exactly who the biological father is. Donor #19867 from the Metroplex Fertility Clinic's sperm bank, where I was inseminated."

More glances between attorneys.

"This is a problem," Claire said.

Gannon agreed. "Under Texas law, any children born during a marriage are *legally* the offspring of the husband, unless and until proved otherwise. Meaning court-ordered DNA tests are going to be necessary."

"Why court-ordered?" Wyatt asked, his impatience matching Adelaide's. "Can't we just have them done on our own?"

"Not if you want them to be part of any legal record," Gannon said. "When DNA tests are court-ordered, a strict chain-of-custody procedure is followed, ensuring the integrity of the samples. Everyone who has contact with them has to sign. This protects against tampering, or ill-use."

Made sense.

"Then court-ordered it is," Adelaide said grimly, as Wyatt nodded.

"Luckily, we can formally request this online." Gannon was already typing. "I'll follow it up with a call to the judge to make sure it goes through immediately."

"While you do that, I'll call my cousin Jackson McCabe, who is chief of staff at Laramie Community Hospital, and ask him to write the medical orders for the blood tests." Claire rose, cell phone to her ear. "And arrange to have them done as soon as possible."

Not that it would matter, Wyatt thought, as Claire stepped into the next room and Gannon, when finished, walked out onto the front porch. They all knew what the tests were going to reveal. Once that happened, he and Adelaide would go their separate ways.

Forever.

UNABLE TO SIT still a moment longer, Adelaide rose, gathered the mugs and took them to the kitchen sink. "I wasn't finished with that," Wyatt called after her.

No one had been, Adelaide knew. But she needed something to do before she exploded with tension. "Hold your horses," she said over her shoulder. "You'll get a fresh mug in a minute, and more hot coffee to go with it. Unless you'd prefer something more dainty." She turned his way to give him a too-sweet look. "Like tea?"

He shot her a deadpan look.

They both knew he hated tea. All kinds.

He didn't like iced coffee, either.

Or at least he hadn't.

What if he had changed?

Then again… Doubtful.

Gannon walked back in, just as she sat four fresh mugs and a platter of cookies on the table. "We've got the court order."

Claire returned, too. "Jackson expedited everything on the hospital's end. The hospital lab will be open until eight this evening, so you can both go over now if you like." She paused. "If you want to write this down…?"

Adelaide plucked a notepad and pen from the charging station, then returned to the table, carafe in hand. She slid the former across the table to Wyatt.

He ignored her helpful gesture. "I'll just type it in." He pulled out his smartphone, gaze trained on the oversize screen, paused again, then brought up the appropriate menu.

Just scribbling the info on paper would have been faster. Then again… "It's probably best,"

Adelaide quipped, in an effort to lighten the mounting exasperation. "No one can read his chicken scratches anyway."

Wyatt squinted at her, his expression partly annoyed and the rest inscrutable.

"Unless something's changed?" she continued, determined to be just as provoking and ornery as he was being.

It hadn't just been the love notes he'd passed to her in class she hadn't been able to decipher. It had been anything and everything he wrote. Worse, he had seemed to take perverse delight in everyone else's frustration. Just as he was enjoying her impatience now. She didn't know why he had to be such a pain sometimes.

"You've taken a class in penmanship…?" she taunted lightly, aware they had temporarily reverted to their worst selves from their teenage years.

"You wish." Smugly, Wyatt looked at Claire, his fingers poised over the keyboard on his man-size smartphone. "Ready when you are."

Barely suppressing her own exasperation, Claire returned to her own handwritten notes. "The tech who's going to be doing the test is Martie Bowman. The outpatient lab is on the first floor of the main building of the hospital, in the east wing. Suite 111."

Wyatt quickly typed in the information. "Do you want to email that to me, too?" Adelaide asked.

"Not necessary," Wyatt said. "I've got it."

He was also as impossibly chauvinistic as ever. Adelaide sighed. "How long until we have the results?"

"They're going to put a rush on it. So three or four days at most."

"What about the rest of it?" Adelaide asked.

"It would be advisable to proceed with the divorce only when the DNA results are back," Gannon said.

Adelaide decided to give it one last try. "Are you sure it has to be divorce? Can't we remedy this mistake—" and it had been a big one, the biggest of her life "—some other way? Maybe just invalidate the marriage on some technicality, or…I don't know…" She was grasping at straws, and she knew it.

Wyatt grimaced. "I agree. I'd prefer to find another way to end this, too."

"There isn't one," Gannon decreed.

"You've not only consummated the marriage, but had children during the term of the union, which has lasted nearly ten years," Claire reminded sagely.

Gannon agreed. "Like it or not, divorce is the only way to dissolve your marriage."

No sooner had Claire and Gannon left them to discuss their pending trip to the hospital lab than a wail sounded on the baby monitor. A second swiftly followed.

Adelaide looked at the alarmed expression on Wyatt's face. Suddenly, she was in no hurry to have cheeks swabbed or blood drawn. At least with him standing right next to her. "I've got to feed the twins, so…" She waved him off. "If you want, you can go ahead to the hospital without us."

He stood firm. "I prefer we all go together. Just get it done."

It wasn't as if they didn't already know the results.

Irritated, she took the stairs quickly, as the cries quickly escalated to a fever pitch. "Well, some things won't wait."

He lagged behind at the foot of the stairs. "How long…?"

Adelaide threw the words over her shoulder. "If you want to make it fast, then give me a hand, cowboy."

Never in a million years did she think he would take her up on the suggestion. By the time she bypassed the tiny master and reached the even tinier room with the twin cribs, the volume had been turned up nearly as loud as their little lungs could go.

Unable to bear to hear her children sobbing,

Adelaide quickly picked up little Jake and snuggled him in one arm. His sobs subsiding, she walked over to Jenny's crib and scooped her up, too. Hence, it was suddenly blissfully quiet, as she carried both to the changing stations set up side by side.

"You're going to change both their diapers simultaneously?" Wyatt lingered in the doorway, the same cautious, awestruck expression he had on his face whenever he saw a new foal.

Except this wasn't one of the cutting horses he bred on his ranch.

Adelaide shrugged. "Neither one of them is all that keen on going second."

"Then how do you…?"

"When I was nursing, I put one on each breast."

She knew it was too much information. She also figured too much information might incent him to leave.

He seemed to know that was what she wanted,

so, as ornery as ever, he strolled languidly into the room.

Jenny and Jake lay on their backs while she worked at unsnapping their onesies, letting their legs go free. Fortunately, both diapers were just wet.

"They look like you," Wyatt said softly.

No surprise there. She had picked a donor with the same shaped facial features, dark wavy hair and bittersweet chocolate eyes as her own.

The tender regard in his expression made him all the more handsome. "Their eyes are blue, though."

Pure blue.

His were blue-gray.

The wistfulness he was suddenly evidencing forced her to recall he had always wanted kids, too. "Most fair-skinned babies are born with dark blue or dark gray eyes that can change color several times before their first birthday."

He stuck his hands in his pockets. "Did not know that."

Did not know a lot of things. Finding it a relief to be able to distract themselves with information, she explained, "An infant's eye color changes as he or she gets older and melanin levels increase."

He watched as Adelaide eased away the wet diapers, quickly wiped down their diaper area and slid on the new.

Wyatt turned to her, his broad shoulder nudging hers in the process. "When will you find out?"

Ignoring the electricity of the brief contact, she fastened one, then the other. "By their first birthday, I'll know if their eyes are going to be blue or brown or green or gray."

Not that it mattered.

They would be adorable regardless.

She turned back to the man she had once loved. Suddenly, he wasn't the only one feeling wistful. Had their elopement worked out, the way they both had hoped, these children could have been theirs. But they weren't. So…

She sighed, aware Wyatt had gone back to observing her children. He leaned closer, regarding them contentedly. For a person who'd had zero interest in ever laying eyes on the two babies she'd had on her own, he was certainly fascinated.

"I think they have your nose, too. See the way it turns up slightly at the end?"

She certainly recalled Wyatt kissing her nose. And her cheek, and her temple, and…

Best she not go there.

She really should not go there.

"Your eyelashes, too," he mused.

Aware this situation was getting far too intimate too fast, she challenged him with a droll look. "Is that a good thing or bad?"

He straightened. As their gazes collided, it was hard to tell what he was feeling.

"Fact."

"Whew!" She pretended to wipe perspiration from her forehead. "For a moment, I thought you were paying me compliments."

His low laugh filled the room, bringing back a slew of unwanted memories.

Simmering with emotion, Adelaide scooped up Jenny in one arm, Jake in her other. She headed down the hall. He followed, close enough she could feel his steady male presence. "You're really going to go down the stairs like that?"

He was a man. Of course he wanted to take charge. "Very carefully. And yes, I am."

He still looked skeptical.

With good reason, had she not already done this dozens of times.

Figuring as long as she had a pair of helping hands nearby she might as well use them, Adelaide turned and handed off little Jake. For a moment, Jake gazed up at Wyatt mutely, studying the handsome rancher's unfamiliar face.

Blinking in confusion, Jake let out a howl loud enough to wake the entire neighborhood.

"Now what?" Wyatt mouthed, looking every bit as panicked as Adelaide had felt the first moment she was confronted with two in the hospital. When all she had ever signed up for was one baby. Until Mother Nature had intervened. Adelaide held out her free arm.

Wyatt slid Jake back into her hold.

To everyone's relief, the crying ceased.

Adelaide continued on downstairs, as originally planned. Once in the kitchen, she had no choice but to put both babies down in their infant seats, as she prepared their bottles. Luckily, they were so focused on watching her, each other and their visitor, both forgot to voice their immense impatience, as per usual.

Wyatt stood next to her, his arms braced on the counter on either side of him. Was it her imagination, or did he look completely besotted by her precious offspring?

"When did you stop nursing?"

"Our doctors made me stop when they reached four and a half weeks. I wasn't able to provide enough milk for both and trying to do so was having an adverse effect on my health." She sighed her regret. "Since I'm all they've got, I had to do what was best for all of us. Even if that meant making concessions I would really have rather not." She paused to give her babies adoring looks. "I thought it might be hard for them, moving from breast to bottle, but they adjusted really easily. Maybe because they were already getting supplemental formula feedings."

He nodded. Understanding in a way she didn't expect.

Telling herself this was no time to start feeling kindly toward him, Adelaide put one bottle in the warmer, waited for it to ding, then added the other. Finished, she tested the liquid of both on the inside of her wrists. Scooping up both babies, she inclined her head at the bottles. "Mind bringing those in for me? You'll save me a trip."

"Sure."

Adelaide walked over to the sofa and settled both infants into the supportive indentions on the extra-large twin nursing pillow already there, then she sat and carefully moved it onto her lap. Wyatt handed over the bottles one at a time, and she tipped the nipples into Jake and Jenny's mouths. Then all was silent as they drank. For the first time in a while, Adelaide felt herself begin to relax and really breathe. Until she looked up again and saw Wyatt watching her with the kind of respect she had always yearned to see.

Telling herself that his newfound admiration didn't matter, that this situation would be over as quickly as their one-night stand had been, Adelaide bent her head and did not look up at him again.

AN HOUR LATER, they were on their way. Thankfully in separate vehicles. Four cheek-swab DNA tests later, they again split up. Wyatt returned to his horses and his ranch. Adelaide took the twins home and thus began the wait for results.

They came in late on the third day.

On the morning of the fourth, she found herself back at the hospital. This time in Dr. Jackson McCabe's office. To her surprise, Wyatt was there, too.

Jackson indicated they should sit, even as Adelaide's palms began to sweat. "I understand you requested this test to disprove Wyatt's paternity of the twins."

Wyatt and Adelaide nodded.

"It proved the opposite. Adelaide Smythe is their biological mother, Wyatt Lockhart their biological father."

"But that's…" Adelaide sputtered. She thought this was just a formality! "I was artificially inseminated before Wyatt and I ever hooked up. So it can't be! He can't be!"

SHE SLANTED A look at Wyatt, who was not moving or reacting in any way.

"Apparently the AI did not take," Jackson explained.

That was impossible. "We used protection when we were together!"

Not because she had felt she needed it, since

she had been convinced she was already pregnant by then, but because she hadn't wanted to stop and explain her circumstances, a move that surely would have spoiled the romantic aura of the evening, as surely as it had the morning after. And she had wanted that one night with Wyatt so very badly. To make up for everything heartbreaking and awful that had come before.

"No birth control method is one hundred percent effective." Jackson handed over two sets of lab results. "The tests were conclusive. Both children are Wyatt's. So—" he rose, reaching across the desk and shaking their hands "—congratulations to both of you."

Chapter Three

Wyatt was still reeling from the news that he was a dad, when his younger sister met them at the door of Adelaide's home, where she had been babysitting the twins. Sage caught the equally shell-shocked look on Adelaide's face. "What happened to you?" Immediately incensed, his sister swung back to him and demanded, "Are you responsible?"

If Sage only knew, Wyatt thought ironically. Feeling joy—that he finally had the kids he had secretly wanted for a long time. And shock—that the woman he'd once thought—erroneously—was the love of his life, was the mother who had provided them.

He had no idea why fate kept propelling them together this way. When it was abundantly clear he and Adelaide could not be more wrong for each other.

Yet there was nothing of the cruel joke of nature when it came to the sweetly slumbering children, he thought, gazing down at Jenny and Jake in reverence and awe.

They were perfect.

And they were his.

As well as Adelaide's…

Oblivious to the ambivalent nature of his thoughts, Adelaide turned back to Sage and made a shushing motion with her hand. "It's complicated," she told his sister.

Sage looked them both up and down. Sighed, as a twinkle came into her eyes. "Isn't it always with the two of you?"

Reluctantly, Wyatt turned away from the

twins, who were still sleeping angelically in their Pack 'N Plays. Eager for some time alone with them, he grabbed his sister's coat and bag and ushered her toward the door. "Thanks for babysitting."

Sage dug in her heels. "I can stay awhile longer if you need me."

Adelaide's expression broadcast the need for privacy. "Wyatt and I have some things we need to discuss."

Which probably, Wyatt admitted grudgingly, should be done before the twins woke up.

"Uh-huh." Sage shrugged on her coat and patted Wyatt's arm. "Be good to Adelaide, big brother."

As if he had ever wanted to be anything but, Wyatt thought grumpily. Even if things hadn't worked out.

Sage shut the door behind her.

Adelaide's small house felt even tinier.

Looking as tense and upset as he felt, she went to the kitchen, stood on tiptoe and pulled out a bottle of Kahlua. Wyatt knew how she felt. He could use a good stiff drink himself. Even if it was barely ten in the morning.

Hands trembling, she made two drinks. Wordlessly, they each took a stool at her kitchen island. "What are we going to do?" she asked in a low, jittery voice, lifting the glass to her lips.

He sipped the concoction of milk, ice and coffee-flavored rum. "The only thing we can. Raise them together."

She looked down her nose at him. "I'm not staying married for all the wrong reasons."

He grimaced as the too-sweet mixed drink stayed on his tongue. "I'm not asking you to stay married," he retorted in exasperation. "I still think we should get a divorce."

"Good." Relief softened her slender frame. "I'm glad we agree on that, because the last thing I want Jenny and Jake to suffer through is a marriage like my parents had," she vowed, her cheeks turning an enticing pink. "With both of them fighting all the time."

He gazed into her eyes. "I promise you. For the sake of the kids, we won't fight." And especially not the way Paul and Penny Smythe had, before Penny had died in that Jet Ski accident when Adelaide was fourteen. He could still remember how unmaternal Adelaide's mother had been, her dad only a little more interested in their only child. Had it not been for the teachers, camp counselors and horse-riding instructors who had taken an interest in the shy but eager to please little girl, he wasn't sure what would have happened to Adelaide.

Her face grew pinched. "I promise you, too. We'll keep things civil in the way we haven't managed to in the past."

Regret tightened his gut. It wasn't the first time he had felt remorse over having given her such a hard time. "Then, we had no reason to buck up," he admitted shamefully.

She nodded, accepting her own culpability in the ongoing tension between them. "Now, we certainly do."

The unmistakable ache in her tone caught him unawares. He studied her, realizing for the first time she might wish that things had turned out different for them, too, despite her avowals to the contrary.

Silence. She lifted her eyes to his, then looked at him long and hard. "The question is, how are we going to arrange it?"

He drained his glass. "I don't want a judge to tell us how the twins are going to divide their time."

She pushed her unfinished drink away. "I don't want them to divide their time at all," she said firmly, sending him a probing look that sent heat spiraling through him. "Not when they are this young."

It took everything he had not to touch her again. Haul her into his arms. And… "What are you suggesting?" he bit out.

She angled her chin. "That we work together to get you up to speed on all the daddy stuff and make you and the twins comfortable with each other."

That sounded good in terms of the kids, but there were still wrinkles to work out. "I'm not moving into my mother's bunkhouse, Adelaide." He anticipated enough family interference as it was. From his mother, who never seemed to trust him to be able to succeed without her help. And his way too idealistic younger sister, Sage, whose own unsatisfying love life prodded her to look outward for her fix of romance.

"Well, we can't stay here. The work on the addition to my home is due to start in two days, and the movers are coming to take the bigger items, like the twins' cribs and changing tables and so on, tomorrow." She rose and carried her glass to the sink.

Wyatt took his over, too. "I don't understand why you just didn't buy a bigger place to begin with when you moved here from Dallas last fall." Their shoulders touched as they leaned over to put the dirty dishes into the dishwasher.

Adelaide shut the lid and straightened. "I thought about waiting until spring, when more properties were likely to be on the market, and renting something else in the meantime, but I also knew that the modest price and the location of the cottage—just blocks from downtown where I work—couldn't be beat. So I put an offer on it that was immediately accepted."

Okay, that made sense, even if his urge to kiss her again did not. "Why didn't you do the addition before the twins were born?"

She raked her teeth across her lower lip. "Because Molly and Chance were both busy with other jobs, and I wanted one or both of them to handle it for me."

That he could also understand. His contractor brother and his fiancée had the best building teams around.

Adelaide moved away, giving him a brief, enticing view of her curvy backside in the process.

She swung back to face him, picking a piece of lint from the knee of her trim black wool skirt.

"I also didn't think the twins would need separate bedrooms for a couple of years. But, given the way they keep waking each other up, I figured it would be better if they each had their own space now. A dedicated space for me to work in, when I do work at home, would be nice, too. And since I was able to get a low-interest construction loan from the bank and Molly and Chance were able to fit my project into their schedule... I went for it."

"Makes sense." Even if it would cause a lot of temporary upheaval.

Adelaide removed the coated elastic band from her wrist, gathered her wavy dark hair into a knot on the back of her head and secured it there. "Unfortunately, the babies can't be around construction dust and fumes. It's not safe."

The good thing about Adelaide was that she could be easily persuaded to do what made sense logically. The bad thing was that she often came to regret her ready acquiescence if the situation did not continue to align with her wants and needs. Still, she was also known for making the best of whatever situation she found herself in. A propensity he knew would be helpful to both of them in the coming months. Briefly he covered her hand with his own. "You and the babies can stay at Wind River with me. I've got plenty of room at the ranch."

She pinched the bridge of her nose and looked even more stressed than she had in Jackson McCabe's office. "That will cause a lot of talk."

Why did people always think gossip was the worst thing in the world? When what really sucked was hiding the truth out of *fear* of scandal. He shrugged. "There's going to be a lot of talk anyway."

Adelaide looked like she wanted to thrust herself against him and hold on to him for comfort. But of course she didn't.

She ran her finger along the edge of the granite countertop. "How are we going to handle that?" she asked anxiously.

Wyatt worked on keeping his emotions in

check, too. This situation was hard enough without adding messy feelings to the mix. He looked Adelaide in the eye. "For starters? By getting my family together."

ADELAIDE COULDN'T RECALL ever being this nervous. "Are you sure you want to do this right now?" she asked, as she bundled up the twins and strapped them into their car seats.

Wyatt grinned, as confident as she was on edge. "Sage already knows something's up. Garrett works at the hospital, so he may have heard we were there with the twins earlier in the week. Then there's the court-ordered bloodwork, the fact that both our attorneys were at your house with us. Singularly, none of those details may have caused much gossip, but all together..."

Trying not to notice how he towered over her when they stood side by side, she shut the rear passenger door.

"Besides—" he rested his big hands on her shoulders "—the fact I have two children, that the twins have a daddy to love and watch over them, is fantastic news."

"You're right." She stepped back, aware having his kids was, in many ways, her deepest held romantic fantasy come true.

She'd never imagined it would actually be possible, though. Or dreamed he would ever be able to forgive her for changing her mind about marrying him. Because it had been more than his pride that had been destroyed that day. Her actions had eradicated his trust in her. And in them. She still wasn't sure his faith in her would ever be resurrected, at least not entirely.

And without that, even becoming friends again would be a challenge.

But, given the situation, there was nothing to do but try to forge some peace.

Go on from there.

THEY TOOK BOTH vehicles out to his mother's ranch, the Circle H. By the time they arrived, the Lockhart family was already there, save

Wyatt's brother Zane, who was on assignment with Special Forces.

The rest were gathered in the main room of the bunkhouse. Garrett and Hope, and her eleven-month-old son, Max. The newly engaged Molly and Chance, and her three-year-old son, Braden. Wyatt's sister, Sage, and his mother, Lucille.

Adelaide settled the twins, who were still fast asleep in their carriers, at one end of the long plank table, while Wyatt asked them all to have a seat toward the other end.

"So what's up?" Sage asked.

Adelaide's pulse raced as Wyatt moved to stand beside her. She hadn't expected to ever want to rely on him again, but right now, she did.

Especially with his family looking at them so curiously.

"Adelaide and I eloped in Vegas on Valentine's Day, when we were eighteen," Wyatt announced, as if it were no big deal.

Brows rose all around.

"We thought we annulled it before we left the state, but apparently we were mistaken."

Garrett cocked his head, clearly as shocked and disbelieving as everyone else. "So you're still married," he concluded.

Adelaide lifted her hand. "Yes, but we're getting a divorce," she clarified quickly.

Wyatt frowned. "Eventually," he said.

Lucille pressed a hand to her heart, her joy surfacing as the reality sunk in. "You're going to give the marriage a try?" The matriarch of the Lockhart clan looked delighted. There was nothing she wanted more, Adelaide knew, than to have all five of her children married and living happily-ever-after.

"No," Adelaide corrected hastily, glad to see that at least Lucille did not look disappointed in them. At least not yet. "But we have to learn how to live together because…" She cleared her throat. Oh heck, she really did not know how to put this.

The man of the hour did.

Casually, Wyatt related, "We hooked up a while ago, at a wedding, when Adelaide thought she was already pregnant via artificial insemination, and long story short—" he couldn't quite suppress a triumphant grin "—we just found out the twins are mine. Ours."

A second really shocked silence reverberated around the table.

Glad to see this, too, was happy news, Adelaide added, with an outer confidence she couldn't begin to feel, "Naturally, we want to do what is best for everyone. So Wyatt and I have decided to join forces and move in together at his ranch, until such a time as we can figure out a way to be a family without being married or living under one roof."

Chance and Garrett exchanged looks. "How long do you expect this to take?" Chance asked.

Adelaide had no clue. The only thing she knew for sure was that she was in no rush to let the twins out of her sight for more than a few hours every day. Given how quickly he was stepping up to the plate, she assumed Wyatt would soon feel the same.

"A year. Maybe more," Wyatt said.

"However long it takes us to consciously uncouple," Adelaide agreed.

Sage tilted her head, looking every bit as happy as her mother, Molly and Hope. "Well, if it works for the Hollywood stars, why shouldn't it work for the two of you?"

Chance and Garrett both guffawed.

"This is serious." Lucille frowned. "Under the circumstances, I think you should both forget about ever getting divorced. And have a proper wedding, here on the ranch, as soon as possible, with all your friends and family present."

The pressure of that kind of public hoopla made Adelaide reel. "Not going to happen, Mom," Wyatt said. A little too quickly for Adelaide's taste.

Was the thought of doing what was best for the twins in the conventional sense really so distasteful to him? Did he hate her that much?

On the other hand, she knew he was certainly being practical in wanting to go into the arrangement with their eyes wide open.

"We should at least have a party to officially welcome Adelaide and the twins into the family," Lucille insisted.

"Once the dust settles on the news, that is probably a good idea," Hope concurred, her considerable expertise as a crisis manager and public relations expert coming into play.

"How do we get the word out?" Sage asked.

Hope smiled. "The usual way—via announcement."

The women promptly went to work. Fifteen minutes later, they had a rough draft of the whimsical announcement. There was a border of hearts, with a stork across the top, carrying two babies, one in pink, one in blue. Followed by the words:

And just when you think you've heard it all...
Nearly ten years ago, on Valentine's Day,

at the tender age of eighteen, Adelaide Smythe and Wyatt Lockhart eloped.

They soon got cold feet. And had it annulled. Until fate intervened, and they met up again on another starry romantic night.

Twin babies and a surprisingly still legal marriage were the result!

Please join us on the Circle H Ranch, on Saturday March 1, at 4:00 p.m., to welcome Adelaide and the twins, Jake and Jenny, into the Lockhart family, and celebrate the unconventional events that brought them all together. And brought all of us such happiness and love.

"It can be a combination belated wedding reception slash baby shower," Lucille decreed.

Wyatt and Adelaide exchanged worried looks. Adelaide was willing to go along to get along, to a point. Not add more deception to the mix. "I think we might want to add something about our plans to eventually amicably divorce," she said. "Otherwise, we will just face even more scandal down the road."

"Nonsense," Lucille huffed. "If you two want to consciously uncouple, that is your business and can be done privately until such time as you are actually ready to divorce. Right now, the emphasis has to be on the twins. They deserve the kind of fairy-tale entry all children merit as they enter this world. When they look back on these events, as they certainly will someday, I want them to see an unconventional beginning brimming with love and joy."

As much as Adelaide wanted to, she could not argue that.

Chapter Four

"Why are they crying?" Wyatt asked in alarm several hours later. He and Adelaide carried both twins in the front door and set the carriers on the sofa.

Adelaide eased Jake out of the straps and hooded jacket and blanket confining him, and handed him to Wyatt to hold. "A lot of reasons." Tossing her own coat aside, she bent to retrieve Jenny from her carrier, too. "They saw a lot of new faces tonight."

No kidding, Wyatt thought. After the news

had set in, everyone in the family had wanted to congratulate them and cuddle the twins. His mom had persuaded them to stay for an impromptu family dinner. He'd agreed as readily as Adelaide. Mostly because he hadn't figured out how to be alone with her yet, under the startling new circumstances.

He wished he had one-thousandth of Adelaide's ease as a parent.

Horses, he knew. Kids, not so much. He'd never had the golden touch with them. Well, except for his nephews Max and Braden. Those little tykes had taken right to him. Maybe because he bore a resemblance to their own daddies...

"Do you think they're still hungry?" He and Jake edged closer to Adelaide and Jenny. His daughter hadn't lessened her wailing, either. "Because they were fed and burped right before we left the ranch." Less than thirty minutes ago. "Their diapers changed, too."

Adelaide inclined her head, indicating he should follow suit. She carried Jenny up the stairs. "I think they're just wound up and over-tired." They moved into the nursery. "Nothing a little walking the floor with them won't cure. Unless…" Adelaide squinted at him thoughtfully. The crying was so loud now she had to practically shout to be heard. "You'd like to go on home now?"

Wyatt shook his head. He had responsibilities now. "I'll stay until they are asleep," he vowed firmly.

She pressed a kiss onto the top of Jenny's head. He did the same with Jake.

"Your horses…?" she asked.

"Troy and Flint, my hired hands, have already taken care of them."

Briefly, Adelaide looked disappointed. As if she'd been counting on his work to take him away from them. Heaven knew it wasn't the first time she'd used an excuse to put distance between them. It stung, just the same.

He told himself her reaction was understandable. Had it not been for the babies they now shared, he would have been out the door hours ago, new dissolution papers filed.

Instead, he was here with the three of them, trying to make sense of what had happened. Figure out how the heck they were going to proceed on a practical level.

It was one thing to promise to care for the kids together.

Another to actually make the situation work.

Luckily, right now, all they had to concentrate on was easing the persistent crying of their children.

He watched as Adelaide shifted Jenny's head onto her shoulder and tried somewhat awkwardly to do the same. While Jenny cuddled sweetly against Adelaide's soft breast, her head resting against the slender slope of her mommy's neck, Jake resisted doing the same. Recalcitrant, he arched his little spine, tilting the back of his neck against Wyatt's gently supporting palm.

Wyatt was tempted to give up, hand his son over. But given the fact that Adelaide had her own hands full, and Jenny was finally starting to settle down, just a little…

Adelaide mouthed the words, "Move him up a little higher. So his head is…"

Wyatt tried. Little Jake arched again. Opened his mouth wider and the largest belch Wyatt had ever heard came out. Followed swiftly by a flood of curdled, really foul smelling sour milk. Like an erupting volcano, the messy goo went all over Wyatt's shoulder, the front of his shirt, inside the collar, onto his neck. Trying not to get it on Jake, too—who was remarkably unscathed by the flood—Wyatt lifted his son slightly away from him, still holding him gently with both hands, and that's when two things happened. Jenny finally fell sound asleep. And Jake spit up again, this time all over the rest of Jake's shirt and pants.

Gently, Adelaide eased Jenny into her crib. The little darling slumbered on.

Wyatt expected Adelaide to reach for Jake, who, now that he'd emptied the contents of his tummy, was looking incredibly sleepy, too. Instead, she disappeared into the hall bath and came back, a damp washcloth in hand.

By then, Jake had put his head on the only other spit-up free zone of his daddy, Wyatt's other shoulder. His eyes were drifting closed.

Adelaide wiped the curdled milk from her son's face. "Want me to take him?" Adelaide murmured softly.

Wyatt shook his head, feeling incredibly proud and relieved he had done what just a few minutes ago had seemed impossible—nearly put his wildly upset son to sleep. "I've got this," he said.

And to his surprise, he did.

ADELAIDE HAD SEEN new dads cuddling babies. But nothing had ever affected her the way the sight of Wyatt, so tenderly cradling their son, did.

Aware she was near tears that if started would not stop, she turned away. She went into the bathroom, grabbed the lone towel off the rack and returned just as Wyatt was easing Jake into his crib. Her son slept on, looking incredibly peaceful and unscathed.

Wyatt, on the other hand, was a mess.

He looked like he'd been hit by a massive eruption of spoiled milk. He had a little bit in the edges of his hair, along his nape. He smelled even worse. She handed over the towel and another damp washcloth. He dabbed ineffectually, smearing spit-up into the terry cloth rather than removing it from his shirt.

She knew exactly how he felt. "I don't suppose you have any clean clothes in your pickup truck."

He shook his head regretfully.

Adelaide winced. She had nothing that would fit, and even worse, the smell of the sour milk was clearly making them both feel ill. "Experience has taught me the best way to clean up is just get in the shower. If you want to do that and toss the clothes out to me, I'll put them in the wash. An hour and fifteen minutes—you'll be good as new."

For a second, she thought he would argue.

A deep breath had him wincing in disgust and simply saying a gruff, "Thanks." He disappeared into the hall bath.

Twenty seconds later, the door eased open. The clothes, soiled towel and washcloth were handed out. Adelaide took them and disappeared down the stairs.

Luckily, the denim shirt, jeans, black boxer briefs and heavy wool socks could all go in one load. The snowy-white T-shirt and towel would have to go in another. Trying hard not to breathe in the stench, she pretreated the stains, added a detergent that was formulated for baby laundry and switched on the machine. Then she went to thoroughly wash her hands.

Wondering what she was going to give Wyatt to wear, which was maybe something she should have figured out before she had him strip down to nothing, Adelaide started back up the stairs.

Then went back down to get a fleece-lined navy lap blanket from the back of her sofa.

Halfway to the second floor of her cottage she realized two things. First, the shower had stopped. And second, in her urgency to get the river of baby vomit off him, she had neglected to give Wyatt something even more important.

A towel.

She hurried all the faster, reaching the upstairs hall and rounding the corner. Wyatt, never one to stand around waiting to be rescued, had quietly begun his own search for the linen closet. Never mind he was dripping wet and smelling of her lavender shampoo, from head to toe, his only clothing a pale pink washcloth that had already been in the shower, held like a fig leaf over his privates.

The ridiculousness of the scene, the sheer unpredictability of their situation, coupled with the sight of all those sleek, satiny muscles beneath the whorls of hair covering his tall body, had her catching her breath.

Memories flashed.

Laughter bubbled up in her chest.

He grinned, too—sheepishly now. But blissfully, kept his hand, and the washcloth, modestly in place.

That, too, hit her, hard.

The laughter came out.

Wilder now.

Uncontrollable.

Then, just as swiftly, turned into loud, wrenching sobs.

The kind that could wake her babies.

Tears streaming down her face, hand pressed against her mouth, smothering the increasingly hysterical sounds, Adelaide stumbled into the master bedroom.

The next thing she knew Wyatt's hands were on her shoulders. Warm. Soothing. He was spinning her around, pulling her close, wrapping his arms around her, holding her tight. And still she cried, and laughed, and cried some more. Her emotions spinning as out of control as her life.

She lifted her head, opened her mouth to jerk in a breath. And then his lips were on hers, drawing her in, and she was as lost in him as she had ever been.

HIS EMOTIONS JUST as out of control as Adelaide's, Wyatt folded the woman who had once been so much a part of his life, even closer. She was soft and vulnerable, feisty and sweet, and when it came to any sort of reconstituted relationship between them, stubbornly resistant as all get out. Yet when he held her in his arms, kissed her with such fierce abandon, she was all yearning, malleable woman. And right now he wanted her that way.

Not laughing and crying as if her world were splintering apart. Not angry and confused at the unexpected twist their lives had taken. And definitely not as furious as he had been since the last time they'd spent a night together, just under a year ago. When she had finally gotten the courage to make love with him. And then left him again anyway.

He didn't ever want her to feel as gut-punched as he had, when he had discovered she had chosen to have a baby with an anonymous donor rather than risk having a family with him.

Only to find out what he had wanted all along had come true anyway.

The undeniable fact was that after all this time he still wanted her, wanted this. Wanted the chances they'd never had. Most of all, he wanted to take advantage of the gifts they had been given. The kids. And through them, another chance, this time to get it right...

He'd half expected her to offer some resistance, even if it was only token. He ran a hand down her spine, pressing his hardness into the softness of her body.

She moaned at the onslaught of pleasure engulfing them both. Lifting his mouth from hers, he strung kisses along her jaw, her nape, the open vee of her blouse.

Lifting her arms to wreathe his shoulders, she pressed against him and kissed him back with a wildness beyond his most erotic dreams. Went up on tiptoe, her hands sliding down his spine, lower, lower still.

His body throbbing, he felt her end the kiss and then watched her step back. Damn if she wasn't the most beautiful woman he had ever seen.

Pink cheeks still wet with tears, dark eyes glowing, she sucked in an impatient breath and shimmied her skirt down her thighs. Toed off her suede flats and stripped off her tights.

He caught her hand before she could remove her blouse, undo the clasp of her bra. "Let me."

Her breath stalled. Holding her arms akimbo, she said softly, her eyes still holding his. "If you insist…"

Oh, he insisted all right.

Her blouse went the way of her skirt, and her skin felt soft and silky beneath his fingers.

Whole body thrumming with need, he undid

the clasp and eased her ivory bra down her arms. Her breasts were fuller than he remembered, taut and round, the nipples rosy and erect. She wore matching panties that were slung low across her hips.

He hooked his thumbs into either side of them and tugged them down. Past the damp curls, her sleek thighs, past her knees. She gasped as he lowered her to the edge of the bed, parted her knees with his hands and buried his face in her sweet warm softness.

"Wyatt…" She caught his head in her hands, quivering now.

"Shhh." He found his way to the feminine heart of her. "Busy here."

She laughed softly. Shakily, as if on the verge of a new flood of tears.

Determined to help her find the release she sought, he dropped butterfly kisses, slow and deliberate.

She shuddered again but did not resist as he ran his thumb along the feminine seam, coaxing her to let all her worries, all her inhibitions float away, to open for him even more. She whimpered low in her throat and gave him full rein. He suckled the silky nub and stroked inside her, fluttering his tongue, until she caught his head in her hands and let her thighs fall even farther apart.

She quivered as he cupped her bottom with both hands, lifted her farther back on the mussed sheets of her bed. Pausing only long enough to grab the condom he carried in his wallet, he covered her and penetrated her slowly. She closed around him like a wet, hot sheath, her entire body shivering with need.

Feeling a little like the conqueror who had just captured the fair maiden of his dreams, he kissed her again, slowly tenderly, even as she draped her arms and legs around him and arched up to meet him. Her response, as true and unashamed as he always hoped it would be, he plunged and withdrew, aware of every soft whimper of desire, every wish, every need.

Until there was no more holding back for either of them.

She came apart in his hands. He free-fell right after her. Together they spiraled into ecstasy, and then slowly, breathlessly returned to the most magnificent peace Wyatt had ever known.

For long moments they held each other tightly, still shuddering, breathing hard. Loving the warmth and softness of her, he rolled so he was on his back. Stroking one hand through her hair, he held her nearer still.

Finally she lifted her head, and her hand came to rest in the region of his heart, even as a wry smile curved her kiss-swollen lips.

"So," she whispered with unexpected playfulness. Ready to do what she always did, which was downplay the import and strength of their connection. "Is this part of our conscious uncoupling, too?"

Chapter Five

"We're really going to throw that term around, as pertaining to us?" Wyatt asked lazily, doing his best to ignore the disappointment churning in his gut.

He knew Adelaide wasn't the least bit romantic. She had made that clear to him numerous times. Part of it was the way she had grown up, with a family that didn't seem to know the first thing about love.

Another was the linear nature of her chosen profession—as an accountant, numbers either added up or they didn't, and if they didn't, there had to be a concrete reason.

The rest was her unwillingness to forgive him for pushing her into an elopement she clearly wasn't ready for when they were kids, and letting her talk him into a reckless consummation years later, when he had known, deep in his gut, she hadn't been ready for that, either.

And tonight they'd done it again.

Made love on a reckless whim. For a whole host of reasons, all of them, obviously, in her retrospective view, wrong. Which likely meant, deep down, she was mad at him. Again. Even if she wouldn't let herself admit that, either.

Adelaide extricated herself from his arms, and grabbing a velvety pink blanket, wrapped it around her as she rose from the bed. "Conscious uncoupling is what we're doing."

He thought about how she looked and felt when she was on the brink, and, despite his effort to be the gentleman he'd been raised to be, got hard all over again.

He waggled his brows. "Funny, that felt more like coupling to me."

"Ha, ha." Adelaide grinned and tossed her head. "And you know what I mean. We have to figure out a way to get along with each other and peacefully co-parent. This—" she waved a hand down the length of her body, then his, before pulling on her bra and panties once again "—can only get in the way of that."

Aware he had nothing to put on save the washcloth he'd utilized earlier, he lounged in the mussed sheets of her bed. "Or make things more pleasant for both of us. After all, we're both healthy human beings in our prime. We have needs."

Bypassing her skirt, she walked to the closet and plucked out a pair of jeans.

He got even more aroused as he watched her draw them seductively up her long, sleek legs.

She wrinkled her nose and met his eyes with her own. A flicker of vulnerability shone in the dark chocolate depths. "Are you seriously using that line on me?"

Wyatt lay back on the pillows and folded his arms behind his head. His pulse amped up as she drew another quick breath. "I admit this isn't an itch that needs to be scratched on a regular basis unless I'm with you. Then…" He watched her draw a sweater over her head, only to get it briefly twisted up over the soft luscious curves of her breasts. "I'll be honest. I do want to forget being celibate." He paused, thinking about how passionately she had responded to him. How sweet and seductive she still looked now. "Can you honestly tell me you don't feel the same?"

ADELAIDE LOOKED AT the expression on his handsome face, the rock-hard muscles on his tall, broad-shouldered frame. A whisper of need swept through her, followed swiftly by a yearning that went soul deep.

"You're right. Normally I'm so busy I don't even have time to think about sex. Not the way

I do when I'm with you," she admitted with a reluctant shake of her head, "and then…"

All common sense was gone.

His eyes drifted possessively over her. "It's chemistry. Right?"

She ran a brush through her hair, restoring order to the silky waves, but could do nothing about the just loved glow of her skin. Flushing, she snatched up the thick shearling-and-velour lap blanket she'd brought up for him and tossed it to him. "Unfortunately, given the fact we're all wrong for each other and you're probably never going to forgive me, yes." She turned her back as he took the hint and rose reluctantly.

"Forgive you for what?" His wheat-blond brow furrowed.

Adelaide led the way to the decidedly less intimate first floor. "Not figuring out what my father was doing before he stole millions from the Lockhart Foundation."

Wyatt followed, blanket wrapped around his

waist. "None of us had a clue about that, Addie, until it was too late," he said softly.

There he went with his nickname for her again. There he went, looking at her like he loved her again.

Ignoring the quivering sensation low in her belly, Adelaide pushed on to the laundry room.

"Or getting cold feet the time we eloped." She plucked his clothes out of the washer and tossed them into the dryer. She caught a drift of his scent, as she leaned past him to punch the speed dry button. He smelled like soap and sex and lavender-scented bed sheets.

He shrugged, as if he'd suddenly found a way to let all that go. His gaze tracked hers, serious now. "We were way too young to even be considering marriage."

True, but…

She recited another reason he would never completely forgive her. "Botching up the annulment."

An affable grin deepened the crinkles around

his eyes. "We hired the wrong lawyer. That was all."

He hadn't been this understanding four days ago.

She recited her most unforgivable sin of all. "Sleeping with you in Aspen without first telling you I already had plans to have a family alone?"

With a satisfied grin, he pulled her into his arms and held her close. "If you hadn't done that, I wouldn't be the father to twins," he said, his smoky blue gaze skimming her intently. "Jake and Jenny would be yours, not ours." He sifted a hand through her hair, tenderly cupped the side of her face. "And neither of us would have any clue just how good we are together, in bed—and possibly out."

Resisting the crazy urge to make love with him all over again, right here in the laundry room, she splayed her hands across the hard musculature of his bare chest. "It sounds suspiciously like you're about to let bygones be bygones."

"On two conditions," he declared.

Struggling to regain her equilibrium, she took a step backward and inhaled a shaky breath. "I'm listening."

He moved closer once again, dimples appearing on either side of his wide smile. "You forgive me for being a jackass where you're concerned, for most of the last ten years."

Her heartbeat quickened at the unexpected culpability in his low tone. She thought about the kisses they had shared and how quickly he had rocked her world. Again. She drew a bolstering breath. Swallowed to ease her parched throat. "I think I can do that."

He lightly caressed the back of her hand. "And we agree not to lie to each other or keep things from each other from now on." He paused to let his words sink in. His expression turned calm, inscrutable. "I'm serious, Addie. Because I can't do this on-off again thing or have you run away and put a stop sign in front of your heart again. Like you did in Vegas. And Aspen," he told her quietly, gaze narrowing. "I don't want to feel like I'm not good enough for you to hitch your future to."

Not good enough! Was he kidding her?

"Where did you get that idea?" Adelaide retorted, unsure whether it was emotion or nerves causing her to respond so emotionally.

Looking impossibly manly with only a blanket knotted around his waist, he shrugged. "You were obviously holding out for something back then." Folding his arms in front of him, he braced his legs a little farther apart. "I kind of didn't think it was something *worse* than what I had to offer."

"Don't joke around," Adelaide said harshly.

Their eyes met and held for a breath-stealing moment. An expression she couldn't read passed across his face.

"Look, I'm okay if you don't love me. I'm not sure I love you anymore, either, or even if I ever did, but I have never stopped wanting you, or wanting to be with you. And if we are going to be together like this, then we have to be all in or all out," he warned, with a tone edged in steel. "Otherwise, I'm going to feel played again and resent you. And the tension between us will be unbearable—and that would be bad for the twins."

He was right about that.

They did need to be honest about what they each desired. Mindful of not just the twins' welfare, but their own feelings, as well.

"All right. I'm all for a physical relationship with you while we are living together. As long," Adelaide said, lifting a cautioning hand, "as it is a bed buddies, no-strings type of thing."

He studied her. "That's what you want?"

No, but it was realistic.

So she would settle for that. Because she had no other choice.

Not trusting her voice, Adelaide nodded.

The reserve was back in his stormy eyes, along with lingering desire. "And one other thing," he said gruffly.

Her heart skittered in her chest.

She braced herself. "Yes?"

"If you have reservations about anything, I want you to tell me, and I promise I will do the same."

"Okay."

As for the rest…

The fact someone had been posting crazy messages on her social media pages, pretending to be her father, and then deleting them as soon as she'd read them…well, she didn't want to go into all that. There were some things that did not bear discussing. Not anymore. Not if they were going to have the peace they all desired.

"WHAT ALL IS going on the truck?" the two local movers asked Adelaide late the following morning, as she cradled Jenny in her arms.

"Everything from the nursery, including the two cribs, changing tables slash dressers, and rocker glider. And…?" Adelaide turned to Wyatt, who was holding Jake. "Do you have a guest bed at Wind River?"

"No."

The thought of them sharing sheets every night was definitely too much, too soon. She wanted them to be co-parents—not feel married. Even though, of course, technically they still were.

"Room for one?"

He tracked the pulse throbbing in her throat. Grinned. "Yes."

A self-conscious flush flooding her face, she swung back to the movers. "You'll also need to bring my bed. And all the assorted baby gear I've stacked in the living room."

Wyatt squinted, as the movers stripped her linens and dissembled her bed. "Sure you want to do that?"

They had made love again and slept together the night before, but that didn't mean they would want to do so every night hereafter. Since he didn't have a guest bed, she would bring her own.

"They aren't going to open up the walls on both floors until the addition is actually framed out. When they do, though, I was advised to cover everything in the vicinity with protective cloths, even though heavy plastic sheeting will be hung in the entryways to keep out the construction dust. Not having my bed there will mean one less thing to cover."

Wyatt wasn't fooled.

He knew she was still keeping one foot out the door and clearly wasn't happy about the idea. However, he might feel differently the first time sharing space got on their nerves. As she was sure it would eventually.

Luckily, they had no more time to discuss it.

The truck was loaded. "We're going to Wind River Ranch, not the Circle H," Adelaide told the crew.

Wyatt gave the address and directions.

And off they went. Adelaide could only hope they were doing the right thing.

HALF AN HOUR LATER, they reached Wind River, the horse ranch Wyatt ran. She'd heard it had been pretty run-down when he inherited it, but it looked to be in good shape now. With a long inviting drive, plentiful tree-lined pastures, outdoor and covered training arenas, and well-maintained outbuildings.

Wondering why Wyatt had parked beside them and directed her and the moving truck to do the same, Adelaide got out of her SUV. "Where's the ranch house?"

Wyatt blinked as if she had asked him the obvious. He pointed to the freshly painted slate-gray barn in front of them.

"You're kidding."

He wasn't kidding.

Upon closer inspection, she saw there were windows on both floors, and the double doors in the center had dark black pulls on them, and a doorbell to one side. "You live here?"

Wyatt rubbed the flat of his hand beneath his jaw. "Surprised you hadn't heard."

Actually, she had heard some jokes from his brothers about him acting like he lived in a barn sometimes, but she thought they had just been razzing him.

Wyatt opened the rear passenger door of her SUV, while she opened the other. "Let's get the twins inside."

She plucked one infant carrier from its base, he undid the other. Together, with the sleeping twins still cozily ensconced in their travel seats, they headed up the walk.

Wyatt opened the door, using the numbered security pad, and held the door for her.

The interior was large and sweeping, sporting a beautiful wide-planked oak floor, creamy white walls, heavy masculine furniture, and dark beams overhead. A living area stood at one end, a kitchen, dining and laundry took up the other. A center staircase—also made of gleaming oak—led to the second floor.

As below, there were abundant windows along the sides and back. At one end of the mostly open space was a king-size bed; the other end held what appeared to be a sparsely appointed home office. A peek into the only walled-off area showed a large steam shower with glass walls, a private commode and a single vanity-sink.

"There's a half bath downstairs, tucked beneath the stairs," he said.

"Very nice," Adelaide murmured, panic beginning to sink in. She looked around. "But where are the twins and I going to be?" Where was her privacy? Her own space? Apart from him, and the desire he aroused in her?

Wyatt shrugged. "Anywhere you want. We can put you where my office is, if you like. Or in the center of the upstairs loft, close to the stairs, if that would be easier. There's plenty of open floor space."

But no walls.

And sometimes, good walls—with doors that shut firmly—made good housemates. No wonder his mother had such reservations about Adelaide and the twins moving in here!

Wyatt stared at her. "You seriously had no idea I lived in a converted barn?"

Adelaide shook her head.

She had tried to learn as little as possible about Wyatt and his life to avoid dwelling on mistakes made and lost opportunities. "Everyone in your family knew better than to try to discuss you with me, or vice versa. It was too upsetting to both of us."

"True."

Adelaide bit her lip. Too late, she realized she should have asked pertinent questions about his home before agreeing to move out here. Since they hadn't begun unloading the truck yet...

She swung back to him, her heart racing. "Sure you don't want to take advantage of your mother's offer and just move into the Circle H bunkhouse, with its six bedrooms and six en suite baths, in the interim?" Her bed could go into storage. Or better yet, back to her home. The twins could each have their own bedroom. Ditto her and Wyatt.

He scoffed, a mutinous look crossing his handsome face. "And have my mother pressuring us daily to make this a real marriage?"

His grim prediction brought her up short. "You're right. It's not what we want," she retorted, just as firmly.

She would go along to get along, just the way she always had.

However, she would *not* make the same mistake she had ten years ago and allow herself to get pressured into a lifelong romantic commitment that she was not ready to make.

Especially when they both knew that a real marriage was the only thing that would satisfy the very traditional-minded Lucille Lockhart.

She and Wyatt could craft a businesslike temporary schedule that included lovemaking—when they both were in the mood—and plenty of time apart, in their own beds, when they weren't so inclined. They could split up care of the kids. That alone would keep them plenty busy.

"We're just doing this for the babies," she said out loud.

His expression unreadable, he nodded. "Because it's the right thing to do for everyone." Wyatt glanced out the windows. "The movers are getting restless. What do you want me to tell them?"

Adelaide carried the still sleeping Jenny to the master bed and set the carrier in the center of it. She motioned for Wyatt to do the same with Jake. "Have them bring everything that was on my second floor up here. We'll just have them set it up in the center for now. My bed on the office side, and the twins' nursery on yours."

Then they would go from there.

"YOU'RE SURE YOU need the bottle warmers?" Wyatt asked later that afternoon, aware how cozy and domestic this all was. And even more surprising how much he already liked it. He paced back and forth, a sleeping Jenny in his arms, watching while Adelaide laid a sound asleep Jake in the Pack 'N Play they had set up.

"If it were just that…" Adelaide reached for Jenny and placed her in the identical bed next to her brother's. Keeping her voice low, she walked back to Wyatt, continuing, "I would wait until tomorrow. But I also forgot the baby first-aid kit and my laptop and work files for my clients, which really shouldn't be left in an unattended home. Plus half a dozen other things we might need, so it's best I go now."

She picked up on his unease. "The twins were awake most of the afternoon, watching the movers and getting acquainted with their new surroundings, so they should sleep most of the next two hours. I can probably be back in a little over an hour. But if you would be more comfortable, I could call your mom. She's just down the road… If Lucille's home, she could be here to help out in five minutes."

The thought of another lecture on why he and Adelaide should just bite the bullet and stay married—for real—instead of trying to figure out how to untangle their lives and successfully co-parent, brought a frown to Wyatt's face. "I've got it," he told her firmly. After all, what could happen in an hour that hadn't already?

Plenty, as it turned out. Jenny woke practically the moment Adelaide's SUV disappeared from view.

No worries.

Adelaide had showed him how to offer a pacifier.

Only problem? Jenny wouldn't take it.

His precious little girl didn't like the fact he was offering it to her, either. She looked around, tears glistening on her lashes, appearing to search for her mommy. And found only him. A poor substitute, in her view. She screwed up her little mouth into a deep frown, glared at him, then let out a howl of outrage.

Ignoring Adelaide's instructions, which had been to offer a pacifier and see if she went back to sleep first, he hastily picked Jenny up.

Too late.

Jake was already awake, as well.

And when he looked around and did not see his mommy, either, he became just as furious as his twin sister. Then proceeded to open his mouth and squall until tears ran down his cheeks.

Meanwhile, Jenny was ignoring all attempts to soothe her and kept on crying as if her little heart would break.

Wyatt had options.

The question was, which should he take?

HER COTTAGE WAS oddly quiet when Adelaide let herself in. Starting the following day, as the foundation for the addition was dug out, framed and poured, it would be pure chaos. But for now with the late-afternoon shadows slanting through the windows and a chill filling the interior, it was almost eerie.

Adelaide shook off her unease and went straight to her laptop. Gloomy atmosphere or not, she needed to check her work email before any more time elapsed. See if there were any crises with clients that would need handling right away.

She booted it up. Waited for her usual screen-saver—a photo of the twins in the hospital nursery, taken just hours after they were born—to come up.

Instead, to her amazement, another photo of a child appeared. Adelaide blinked at the image of herself, at age six, with both her parents, and then another, when she graduated from SMU, in cap and gown, standing with her very proud dad.

"What in the world...?" Adelaide gasped, as the pictures she was looking at disappeared right before her eyes, and the picture of the twins that should have been there all along popped up behind the usual icons.

Adelaide continued staring at the screen.

Had she really seen what she thought she had? she wondered in alarm. If so, how was that possible? Or was whoever had been messing around on her social media pages, posting then removing messages as soon as she'd read them, playing even more tricks on her?

There was only one way to find out. With shaking hands, she reached into her purse and pulled out a card that a local law-enforcement officer had given her when she'd moved to the area. Dialed.

Short minutes later, Kyle McCabe, deputy detective in the Laramie County Sheriff Department, arrived at the house. He'd been off duty when she called but had headed right over.

While the head of their cyber crimes unit set down his messenger bag and shrugged out of his jacket, Adelaide briefly explained what had happened. "It was just there for a second. I almost think I imagined it." But she knew she hadn't.

Kyle examined the programs running on her laptop. "Did you put a remote log-on on your computer?"

"No!"

"Well, someone has. And it looks like the IP address is from Venezuela."

Her pulse began to pound. "How long has it been on there?"

He pointed to the installation date on the screen.

"That was when I was in the hospital, giving birth to the twins."

He studied her. "You're not surprised."

Adelaide told him about the messages she'd received on her social media pages that had also disappeared as soon as she had read them.

"When did they start?"

"Shortly after I got home from the hospital. I had posted Jake and Jenny's photo on my Facebook page and Instagram accounts, and I got a reply that said, 'Twins! I am so proud!'"

"And the post simply disappeared?"

"As soon as I read it. Then I got another a few weeks later that said, 'It was never my intention to leave you behind.' That one just came out of thin air one night when I was getting ready to upload some new pictures on my Instagram page, and again disappeared as soon as I read it. I was so sleep deprived at the time, so torn up over my lack of any real extended family I thought maybe I had dreamed it."

Kyle attached a device to her computer and began making a high-speed copy of all the data. "Why didn't you call me?"

Adelaide shivered and began to pace. "I was hoping that if it really had happened, and again, I wasn't entirely sure it had, that it was just one of the crackpots that harassed me after the scandal with the Lockhart Foundation first broke."

She paused, regretfully reflecting on the many hateful comments that had initially caused her to shut down all her social media until after the birth of the twins. When she had hoped enough time would have elapsed for it to be safe from harassment again.

"Were there any others?"

Reluctantly, Adelaide stopped and turned. "I received the last one two weeks ago." *Well before her life had imploded with the news she and*

Wyatt were not only still married but shared twins. "It said, 'We can be part of each other's futures.'"

"You think it was him?"

Adelaide shrugged. "It certainly wasn't Wyatt." She massaged her forehead. "Sorry." She didn't know why she had just blurted that out.

Kyle smiled sympathetically. "Congratulations, by the way."

Adelaide flushed. She still found it embarrassing to have everyone know that she and Wyatt had slept together. "Thanks."

"Does Wyatt know about any of this?"

Her personal misery increasing tenfold, Adelaide shook her head. "He was so angry before. I didn't want to mention it."

"And you shouldn't," Kyle said firmly. "If these messages are from your father, we don't want anyone outside the cyber crimes unit here having a clue."

The low warning in his voice got to her. "You

don't think my dad would mean me and the twins any harm?"

"Not from the sound of it, but he could still inadvertently put you in legal jeopardy for aiding and abetting."

"I've already told you," Adelaide choked on another wave of bitterness. "If I ever see him again, I'm turning him in."

Kyle nodded appreciatively. "In the meantime, the sheriff's department needs to keep the GPS tracker on your phone and SUV, and I'd like to put a keystroke recording device on your laptop, too. That way, if there are any other remote log-in attempts on it, we'll get an immediate alert down at the station, and we'll be able to record and track the activity on our surveillance system in real time."

Adelaide swallowed, as her next thought hit. "You don't think my father…he wouldn't be back in the country, would he? Not without being detected?"

"The Texas-Mexico border is porous. With

fake ID, a change in his looks, yeah, he could do it."

"But why?"

"Maybe he just wants to see you and meet his grandkids. You are all the family he has, you know."

"He has Mirabelle Fanning," Adelaide reminded him bitterly.

"If they're still together. Once a crime is committed, the co-conspirators often split up."

Adelaide thought about that, and knew it wouldn't make any difference to her if they had. She was never going to be able to forgive her father for what he had done. "Or maybe he wants me to steal for him. Or he wants to steal *from me.*" Angry tears blurred her eyes.

"Check your bank accounts and credit cards."

Adelaide sat and quickly pulled everything up. She breathed a sigh of relief. "My accounts are all fine."

"Clients?"

She relaxed even more as she realized none

of those files, which had elaborate security protecting each and every one, had been breached. "Also fine."

He opened his leather messenger bag. "I'd like to sweep the house and then put some listening and recording devices in."

Adelaide envisioned a team of law-enforcement personnel storming her house, much as they had in Dallas after the initial scandal broke. The fact she had requested their presence to see if they could find anything there had not made it any easier to bear. "Won't that cause a lot of talk?" Talk that would be sure to get back to Wyatt and the rest of the Lockharts?

"If I do it while you're still here, no one will be any wiser."

Adelaide watched as Kyle put tiny devices behind pictures, under lamps. Another minuscule camera was trained at the front door. "People could wonder why you're staying so long."

Early evening, Kyle had already been there an

hour. While Wyatt was back at the ranch with the twins. Who, most likely, were still sleeping.

Casually, Kyle provided their cover story. "If anyone asks, you're doing my taxes for me."

Made sense. She was a CPA who often met with clients at her home.

Kyle cast her a brotherly look. "It'll be okay, Adelaide."

"Good, because I really can't afford to be at the epicenter of another scandal right now. Nor can the Lockharts. And if this turns into a mess…"

Kyle guessed where she was going with this. "You could easily find yourself in the middle of a custody battle."

Adelaide nodded miserably.

Kyle walked into the attached garage and put a device just above the back door. "Wyatt's a good guy."

Adelaide knew that.

But like her, he wasn't without his faults. "Just not the most forgiving type. Which is," she said, squaring her shoulders and drawing a deep breath, "another reason why I don't want Wyatt to know. We're trying to become a family right now…"

"Nothing will be leaked from the department," Kyle promised.

"That's good," she said in relief. Because she was pretty sure if her dad was back, Wyatt would not understand. Or forgive.

Chapter Six

Adelaide hoped to find peace upon her return to the ranch. And, thankfully, the converted barn was quiet, except for the whisper of the double-stroller wheels gliding across the wide plank floor.

It was Wyatt who looked on the verge of parental exhaustion, a feeling she knew all too well.

Guilt mingled with regret. Wondering just how long he had been pushing the stroller around, she set down her belongings and quickly shrugged out of her coat. "Sorry that took so long," she said, moving toward him.

He stayed where he was, gently moving the stroller back and forth. Nodded, as if to say, "I'll bet."

She hated withholding stuff from him, had sworn she wouldn't do so again, and yet here she was, forced, for all their sakes, to hide what was really going on with her.

Aware Wyatt always noticed much more than she wished, she closed the distance between them. "I got caught up. I had a problem with my laptop, which—" she sighed in real frustration "—I was eventually able to resolve. And then Kyle McCabe dropped by." She choked out the fib, knowing that if her "husband" heard about it, it should be from her. "He wants me to do his tax return."

"You couldn't have called?" Wyatt asked brusquely.

Of course she could have, but she had needed the time to gear up for the half-truths she was going to have to tell if she were to keep him—and the twins—out of the mess her life was quickly becoming. "You're right. I should have."

He gave her a telling look but made no reply.

She knelt to look at her little darlings. "What's been going on?"

Seeing her, both babies spit out their pacifiers and burst into tears. With a *shhh* sound, Adelaide steered the stroller to the rocker-glider. She put on the brake, sat, then gathered first Jenny, then Jake into her arms, cuddling them against her breasts.

"They've been awake the entire time," he reported grimly, his emotional exhaustion mirroring hers in similar situations. "The only thing that soothed them was that." Looking tough and sexy in his usual indomitable way, he pointed to the stroller.

As Adelaide rocked the twins, slowly, but surely, their cries subsided. "So you've been wheeling them around the entire time?" *For three hours?*

"When I wasn't changing them and feeding them another bottle, which by the way, neither seemed to really want."

She hated that he'd had such a hard time. She allowed herself to admire the width of his shoulders and the flex of his muscles beneath his shirt. "Why didn't you call me? Or your mother?"

Wyatt's brow furrowed. "I didn't call my mother because she already lacks faith in my ability to do this on the fly."

Adelaide knew Lucille could hover. Particularly where her Wyatt was concerned, but she had never realized it bothered him. "Did Lucille do or say something…?"

He was silent a long moment, his expression inscrutable. "She emailed me a slew of articles on being a good dad and husband."

Adelaide swallowed around the sudden ache in her throat. "Husband?"

"Yep."

The tension within her intensified. Only it was a different kind of heat and tension. The kind that usually preceded their lovemaking. "Lucille knows we're not planning to stay married."

His gaze caressed her face. "Yeah, well, she says the key to being a good father is being a good husband. So, according to her, if I really want to do it right, I've got to figure out a way to make us work, too."

"I'm sure she means well," Adelaide soothed.

He cocked his head. "I take it this means you didn't get any articles?"

"Ah. Not yet." *Hopefully never.* "But," Adelaide said, trying to stay positive, "even if she did send them, I would not take offense because your mom has become a second mother to me."

In fact, Adelaide wasn't sure what she would have done the last year without Lucille. "I'm sure it's just her way of helping," she continued.

He rested his hands on his waist and gave her a dubious glance. "Well, here's hoping Mom offers a lot less assistance in the future."

Adelaide watched him walk into the kitchen and pour himself a glass of chilled water from the outside spigot on the fridge. Big body tense with frustration, he drained two-thirds of it in one gulp.

"Okay, I get why you didn't call Lucille when you could have used some help with the twins," Adelaide persisted, curious, "but why didn't you call me?"

He drained the rest, then looked at her over the rim of his glass. "Because I thought you'd be home any moment."

Home. Adelaide liked the sound of that, despite her inner caution not to let herself get as wound up in her relationship with Wyatt as the Lockhart matriarch wanted.

He let out a rough exhalation of breath, oblivious to her simmering guilt and tension. "And I didn't want to worry you if you were driving." He edged closer, peering at the snoozing babes. "Especially since things were sort of under control," he admitted softly.

Adelaide stopped rocking long enough to

meet his smoky blue gaze. "You did a good job with them."

He sent her a skeptical glance.

"Seriously. With anyone else they didn't really know, if they'd been awake that long, they would have been howling at the tops of their lungs when I walked in. The fact they stayed calm must mean—" she drew a deep breath, determined to get this out whether he wanted her to or not "—they realize on some instinctive level that you're their daddy."

He paused. "I doubt—"

"Can't you feel the connection? With me...in the hospital...it was innate."

He hunkered down beside her, his expression one of almost unbearable tenderness. Reaching out, he gently stroked the side of each baby's cheek. "Yeah." He surprised her by admitting softly, reverently, "I felt it the first time I saw them at your home, even before we had any idea they were ours. That's why I couldn't stop looking at them. And noticing everything about them. I feel it even more now. I just didn't know *they* did."

"Well, they do," Adelaide said fiercely. Powerful emotion welled within her for this man, the children they shared.

"And if you'll help me now, I think we can put them down in their cribs. At least for a little while."

"How do you feel about brisket tacos?" Wyatt asked, when they came back downstairs.

Glad the tension had eased between them once again, Adelaide smiled. She took a seat at the island while he moved around the counter. "Love 'em."

He pulled an armload of items out of the fridge. "Good, because I'm starving, and that's all we've got for dinner that can be ready in about ten minutes. What's that look for?"

Adelaide shook her head in a mixture of apology and regret. "I'm usually so linear about planning, but all I thought about this morning was making sure I had enough supplies to feed and diaper the twins."

"That's why you have me," he joked.

She wished it were true. That he was there to see to her needs and wants, as well as just the twins. But that wasn't the deal they had made.

"I guess you have to be prepared out here in the country." She rested her chin on her up-raised fist, and watched him chop up a pound of smoked brisket, then slide it into a skillet. A smattering of southwestern spices and splash of beef broth followed.

Apparently Sage wasn't the only chef in the family, she thought as the tantalizing aroma of Tex-Mex soon filled the air. "You can't exactly call for takeout."

He flashed her an impish grin. "Not unless you want to drive an hour round-trip to pick it up."

As the mood began to lighten, she found herself relaxing, too. Maybe this arrangement of theirs would work out after all. "Next time I'm in town, I'll check with you before I leave."

He set another skillet on the stove and began warming flour tortillas. While he worked, he poured grated Monterey Jack cheese and slaw into serving bowls. Then got out some chips and tomatillo salsa. "When do you need to go back in to Laramie?"

She dipped a crispy corn chip into the fragrant salsa. "The twins have their two-month checkup next week."

"Can I go?" He helped himself, too.

Adelaide savored the spice on her tongue. "You are their dad."

He grinned, obviously liking the sound of that.

"But yes, to answer your question more directly, I really would like your help," she admitted, the heat in her mouth nothing compared to the heat rippling through her, whenever he neared.

He looked at her, listening intently.

"They're going to have immunizations," Adelaide continued. "And I'm a little nervous about it. The Hep B injections they had at one month didn't go so well."

Wyatt put the softened tortillas in the warmer, turned off the heat under both skillets and covered the meat mixture with a lid. Then came around to sit beside her. "What do you mean?"

Their blue-jeans-clad legs nudged as they faced each other. "Well," Adelaide confessed, a little embarrassed, as he took her hand in his, "they'd never had a shot before. And they cried. And then I cried." Adelaide welled up just thinking about it. "I was supposed to be calm and reassuring, and instead I was almost as much as a mess as they were. At least for a couple of moments. Luckily, your mom had offered to go with me to help out, and she was much more composed."

Wyatt tightened his hand on hers. Stood, and guided her off the stool and into his arms. "That was nice of her," he murmured, stroking a hand through her hair.

Adelaide rested her head against his shoulder. "That's when I got the idea to ask her to be their godmother. Even though what I really wished—" Wyatt's understanding glance helped her admit "—was that Lucille was their grandmother."

He pressed a kiss onto the top of her head. "Looks like you got your wish," he commented in a low gravelly tone. He pulled her tighter against him, his gaze warm, possessive. Sliding his hands down her hips, he planted his hands on either side of her, trapping her between the counter and his tall hard frame. "And for the record, I'm glad we gifted my mother with two more grandchildren, too."

His head slanted downward, and he gazed deep into her eyes. Then his lips shifted over hers, as he delivered the kiss they'd been avoiding all day. Adelaide knew they should slow things down. Get to know each other again first before attempting intimacy. But she couldn't do that this time any more than she had been able to the last time he took her in his arms.

She'd been frightened today.

And she still felt unnerved.

Holding and kissing him felt safe.

Wreathing her arms about his shoulders, she opened her mouth to his and kissed him back with all the pent-up emotion of the day.

Not just once. But again and again.

Sensation swept through her. And suddenly everything she had held back, everything she wanted and needed, came pouring out of her. And what she wanted most was a do-over with Wyatt.

Maybe they couldn't go back to the innocent place where they had left off. But they *could* re-place the heartbreak they'd felt when they split with happier memories. They could use the erotic connection they had to deepen the bond between them.

So she kissed him feverishly, until their hearts pounded in unison. Until her mind was rife with all the possibilities she had been forcing herself not to consider. The God's honest truth was, she wanted to be more than just co-parents with him. Or casual partners. How crazy was that?

As if sensing the direction her thoughts were going, he unbuttoned her blouse, undid the clasp on her bra. Then stepped closer again and kissed her until her breasts pearled and her knees weakened.

His eyes dark with desire, he cupped her breasts and ran his thumbs across the jutting crests. She caught her breath as he ran his hands over her ribs, unzipped her jeans, eased them— and her panties—off, too. The next thing she knew, he had shifted a knee between her thighs. Still kissing her, he showed her a new way of giving and receiving pleasure.

That quickly, she trembled on the precipice. All because of his lips and hands and rock-hard thigh. She moaned again. Pushed him away. "I want us to come together."

He grinned. Grasping both her wrists, he pinned them on either side of her, kissed his way down to her breasts, languidly exploring her nipples. "We can do that, too…"

Impatient to feel him all the way against her, she wrested free, undid his jeans, stroked him silkily. He extracted a condom from his wallet, then tensed as she helped him roll it on. The next thing she knew, he'd lifted her onto the counter. Hands circling her hips, he tugged her toward the edge.

Their eyes locked. Desire and something else…something a lot more powerful…reigned. Her muscles tautened, trembling as he found his way home in one slow, purposeful slide.

Allowing her the time to adjust to the weight and size of him, he went deeper still. Kissing her, rocking into her, slowly, patiently, until she writhed in ecstasy with each stroke. Surrendering to him completely, until there was nothing but the intense driving need, the giving and the taking. Nothing but pleasure and a sweet, swirling oblivion that led to the most magnificent peace Adelaide had ever known.

Gradually, their breathing eased.

Their bodies stopped shuddering.

Adelaide had never felt more like a woman—*his woman*. Shaken by how emotional she felt, she knew she had to change the mood to a much more practical level before she ended up doing something really reckless, like fall in love with him all over again. She opened her eyes and lifted her head.

He looked just as besotted as she felt. "Wyatt?"

"Hmm?" His gruff, sexy voice made her quiver all over again.

She took a deep breath and squared her shoulders resolutely. "That food smells really good. And I'm starving."

WYATT WASN'T SURPRISED Adelaide wanted to put their lovemaking into the Just Sex category. The part of him that had crashed and burned in his prior relationship with her wanted that, too. It would be so much easier. Especially now that they had kids to consider. So, with an easy smile, he conceded to her wishes. Concentrated simply on enjoying their dinner.

By the time they finished, the twins were awake again. Two sets of hands for the diaper changes, and the bottle warmers she'd brought back with her, made quick work of heating up the formula and settling down to feed the babies.

The only problem was, Wyatt noted in disappointment, that neither Jenny nor Jake really wanted him to be the parent caring for them. Both much preferred to be in Adelaide's arms, in their sole rocker-glider. He couldn't really say he blamed them. She was a far sight more adept at all of this than he was. Hopefully, though, with her help, that would soon change.

In the meantime, they had important matters to discuss. "I forgot to tell you earlier. Gannon Montgomery called while you were gone."

Adelaide gestured for him to head up the stairs, toward the "nursery" now set up in the center of the open loft. "And...?"

Aware Jenny was increasingly drowsy, she put

their daughter on the changing table and swaddled her.

Watching, learning, Wyatt paced back and forth, Jake curled up against his chest, peering over his shoulder.

Not sure if it was too soon to discuss this or not, Wyatt told her, "Gannon wanted to know if we are considering any kind of name change for the twins."

Adelaide took Jake and put him on his changing pad, then handed off Jenny to Wyatt to cuddle. Her brow pleated in wary confusion. "You mean call the twins something other than Jake and Jenny?"

"No." Wyatt breathed in the baby-fresh scent of the infant in his arms, not sure when he had ever felt as happy as he did in this instant, with a family of his very own. No wonder all the women he knew, his age, were so baby crazy. He looked Adelaide in the eye, glad she had given him this gift, even if she hadn't actually meant to do so. "Their first names suit them perfectly," he said sincerely.

"Good. For a moment, I thought…" Adelaide broke off with a shake of her head, then slid a folded blanket beneath their son and swaddled him, too.

Wyatt knew Adelaide feared he would barge into their lives, like a bull in a china shop, and try to control everything. Which was why he was trying so hard to give her as much space as she needed, so she wouldn't instinctively withdraw and put up a wall around her heart again.

A move that would make things difficult for them on every level.

"But I would like them to carry the surname of Lockhart," he continued, forthright.

Adelaide picked up the yawning Jake and walked over to gaze out the windows overlooking the south end of the ranch. "How would you feel about a hyphenated last name?"

Wyatt joined her and turned the not quite as drowsy Jenny, so she too could enjoy the sweeping views of the training rings and moonlit pastures that held his cutting horses during the day.

"Smythe-Lockhart?" He tried it on for size.

Adelaide paced toward the area where his office had been set up, and now contained her queen-size bed. It had been placed beneath the arched windows that overlooked the drive leading up to the ranch.

Noting she looked as weary as he felt, he admitted, "I'd prefer Smythe as a middle name, for both, and Lockhart for the last. It's more traditional, especially in rural areas like this. But if you object..."

"I don't." Adelaide carried the now snoozing Jake to the crib. She laid him gently on his back and turned on the musical mobile. The upstairs was suddenly filled with the soothing Brahms lullaby. She took Jenny from Wyatt's arms, settling her in her crib, on the other side of the twin changing tables, beneath her mobile, too.

Straightening, she continued, "The name Smythe still carries negative connotations.

Whereas 'Lockhart' will open a lot of doors for them."

They moved slightly back, away from the well-separated cribs. Watched as the children's lashes slowly closed. "So we're agreed?" he asked softly.

Adelaide nodded, looking as relieved as he felt that the twins were finally asleep. "We are."

UNFORTUNATELY, THE QUIET didn't last. Jenny woke at 9:00 p.m. and roused her brother. They got back to sleep by ten, only to have the reverse happen at eleven. Again, she and Wyatt were able to get both twins asleep by midnight.

The moment they tried to set them in their cribs, however, Jenny and Jake kicked up a fuss that continued for the next two hours.

Both were given bottles, burped, changed and held.

And absolutely nothing worked. The twins were determined not to fall back asleep. Finally, at two in the morning, Wyatt declared, "We tried it your way all evening. Now let's try mine."

He wasn't exactly the expert here. She was. "They are not going to fall asleep."

He oozed testosterone. "We'll see."

Her heart skittered in her chest. "Where are you going?"

"To set things up."

Leaving her in the rocking chair, with both babies in her arms, he bolted up the stairs. She heard him moving around, back and forth, from one end of the loft to the other. From the sound of it, moving the cribs, too. Finally, he came back down. Clad—like her—in pajamas this time. The flannel pants fit loosely. The long sleeved dark T-shirt hugged every masculine muscle. The sight of him, ready for bed, made her mouth go dry.

Luckily, there would be no more lovemaking tonight. Not, given what they were dealing with. And that was a good thing. Wasn't it?

Oblivious to her unexpectedly amorous

thoughts, he eased Jake from her arms. Helped her to her feet. "Follow us, ladies."

With Wyatt in the lead, they mounted the stairs.

Every pillow—and there'd been half a dozen of them—had been removed from her bed and piled against the headboard of his. The cribs had been repositioned, one on either side of his king, at the head of the bed.

Once again, he saw much more than she would have liked. He gazed indulgently down at her. "What's wrong?"

"I was trying to approximate their nursery at home. The problem is, without walls separating the rooms, the acoustics are so different. They may not be able to see things are so different here, but they can hear it and feel it."

And then, there was the lack of privacy she had, too. The feeling she was oh so vulnerable.

He sauntered closer. Leaned down to kiss her temple.

"Maybe what they need to see is Mommy and

Daddy. Sleeping peacefully—or at least pretending to sleep—nearby."

Aware he was going to be very hard to resist, if he kept up the charm offensive, she drew a breath. "So what's the plan, Daddy?"

He grinned at the endearment. "We stop rocking and singing and walking the floor with them. Get into bed, relax and let them snuggle against our chests."

She refused to get sucked in by the blatant sexiness of his gaze. "And then they will magically go to sleep," she countered dryly.

He grinned, optimistic, his wishful thinking stronger than ever. "Probably not right away, but eventually."

At this point, they had absolutely nothing to lose. Except maybe the last of the emotional distance between them.

Tossing a sassy look his way, Adelaide sat on the side of the bed. She swung her legs around and eased back onto the pillows, a swaddled Jenny still in her arms. Wyatt did the same with Jake. They lounged side by side, their legs stretched lazily out in front of them, shoulders, necks and heads nestled comfortably against the heap of pillows.

Unable to help herself, Adelaide let out a long, easy breath.

He nudged her arm playfully. "Feels good, hmm?"

You feel good, pushed up against me like that.

Plus, his sheets smelled like the masculine soap and shampoo he used. Well, that and him. And her pillows smelled like her perfume. The comingling of the scent brought even more sensual memories to mind.

It was a good thing they both held a baby in their arms.

Because otherwise…given the fact this was her very first time to ever climb onto his bed with him…

"Wyatt?" Adelaide lazily tracked the moonlight sifting through the loft.

"Hmm?"

She yawned, suddenly worrying. With sex out of the equation and her baby snuggled in her arms… "This is suddenly making me very, very sleepy."

Wyatt nodded. "Jenny and Jake, too."

Surprised, Adelaide looked down. Sure enough, the twins were nestled against Adelaide's and Wyatt's chests, their faces turned into their necks. Eyes closed, rosebud lips pursed, they were the picture of sweetness and innocence.

Adelaide yawned again, really struggling now. "It won't last," she predicted in a weary whisper, "once we put them down."

He elbowed her lightly again. "'O ye of little faith.'"

Rising ever so carefully, he eased off the bed and placed Jake ever so tenderly in his crib. Then watched as Adelaide reluctantly did the same.

Jenny barely stirred.

Jake slept on.

Adelaide stood there, looking down.

Wyatt took her hand. Drawing her back down, this time between the sheets. "They need to see us if they do wake up, remember?" he whispered in her ear.

Nodding, Adelaide relented. She turned toward Jenny's crib. Wyatt climbed in and turned toward Jake. Spines touching from shoulder to hip, they watched and waited for the next interruption of restful peace.

Chapter Seven

"I don't understand why it's not working," Wyatt said five hours later, when they again tried and failed to put the fed, changed and lightly sleeping twins down in their respective cribs, which had been moved to the right and left sides of his king-size bed.

Seven in the morning, he should be out working with his horses. Instead, he and Adelaide were still trying—fruitlessly—to resituate Jake and Jenny. So Adelaide, at least, could get a few more hours of much-needed sleep.

She sighed and ran her hand through the tousled strands of her dark hair. "I think it's because it's daylight and they can see they're in a strange place."

"You think they'll go back to sleep if we put their cribs elsewhere?"

She drew a breath that lifted the soft curves of her breasts. "I think it's a worth a try."

He tried not to think how intimate it felt, to be standing there with both of them in their pajamas. Or how much he loathed moving furniture on a whim. "Where do you want them?"

Adelaide pointed. "Next to your office area."

"Both cribs?"

"Separated by the changing tables, yes."

Hadn't they already tried that? In the middle of the open second floor, the previous night? Only to have Jake and Jenny continuously wake each other up?

Adelaide set Jenny in her crib. "Putting their

beds next to the light-colored walls might make it seem cozier and more familiar."

Wyatt put Jake in the same bed, next to his twin.

The two babies now sobbed in unison.

Together, she and Wyatt carried the other crib to the far end of the loft. "Here?" Wyatt asked, as the sound of the babies crying lessened the farther they got away.

Adelaide raked her lip with her teeth, surveying the space. "I think we should move both cribs in that corner, where it's not so bright. But it means we're going to have to move your desk a little bit."

Wyatt moved one end of the heavy desk.

"It's crooked."

But there was now room. He waved off her objection. "Doesn't matter."

"But…"

"I don't want to have to unplug everything," he said tersely.

She stepped back. "Oh."

Aware they were on the brink of having their first "marital tiff," he softened his tone and suggested gently, "Let's just move the cribs where you want them now. If it works, we'll worry about finalizing the details later."

Together, they moved one crib, and two changing tables to the corner. "Better?" he asked.

She nodded. Listening. Her brow furrowed as they locked gazes. "Did they stop crying?"

Not sure whether that was a good or bad sign, they both turned and moved to the side of the remaining crib.

"Well, what do you know," Wyatt murmured, as they stared in disbelief.

Jake and Jenny had both wiggled themselves out of the top of their swaddling. Their little hands were outstretched to each other, fingers touching. Heads turned, they were cooing drowsily.

"Amazing," Adelaide whispered proudly.

Wyatt wrapped his arm around her shoulders and tucked her against his side. He wanted to memorize this moment forever. "They really are."

And it wasn't just the twins.

This whole arrangement. Adelaide. It was all remarkable, too.

JAKE AND JENNY fell asleep shortly thereafter. Adelaide and Wyatt decided to take advantage of the quiet to shower and dress for the day. Adelaide showered first, then went down to the first floor, while Wyatt had his turn.

She had just finished drying her hair when she heard a car in the drive. A look out the windows had her opening the door to Lucille, Sage and Hope.

All three were carrying gifts. Lucille and Sage both had wind-up infant swings. Hope had a large basket of baby toiletries and toys.

"We figured it wasn't too early," Lucille said.

Glad to be welcomed so warmly into the Lockhart family, Adelaide ushered them in. "Not at all."

Wyatt walked down the stairs to join them. His hair was damp, his shirt buttoned but untucked over his jeans. He looked sexy and approachable. Tired, but happy, too. "What's up?"

"We brought you something to make your life a little easier," Lucille said, as she and her only daughter set the swings down, side by side.

"All my friends with babies love them," Sage added. "They tell me it's a surefire way to ease crankiness and put a fussy infant to sleep."

"I just wish I'd had one when Max was small," Hope said.

"Of course, sometimes only rocking will do," Lucille continued. She eyed the rocker-glider Adelaide had positioned on the first floor, then looked at her son.

"Don't worry, Mom," Wyatt said dryly. "I'm spending time there, too."

Lucille paused, clearly worried. "If you need advice…"

Briefly, her son looked irritated. "We've got

it covered, Mom." He gestured amiably. "So if that's all…"

"Actually," Hope put in, suddenly looking very much like the crisis manager she was, "we need to talk to you."

Adelaide recognized trouble when she saw it. Had another computer been surreptitiously hacked with remote log-in software? "Did something happen at the Lockhart Foundation?" she asked nervously.

Wyatt sent her a look.

"This time," Hope said gently, "the scandal revolves around the four of you." She handed over a multipage printout containing the recent headlines from Texas gossip and parenting blogs and websites.

Scandal Rocks One of Texas's Famous Families Again! stated *Texas Weekly* magazine.

Surprise—It's Not Just a Decade-Old Elopement, but Twins! blasted the *Dallas Morning Sun* society page.

The popular Lone Star Mommies blog ran with, Parenthood with Both Feet Out the Door?

"And last but not least from the salacious but widely read *Texas Grapevine Online*," Hope said, while Wyatt and Adelaide read with increasing dismay: *Lucille Lockhart, disgraced former CEO of the Lockhart Foundation, had what she terms a happy surprise. Adelaide Smythe, the daughter of longtime family friend and embezzler Paul Smythe, former CFO of the Lockhart Foundation, secretly eloped with her son, Wyatt, nearly a decade ago. Flash-forward to a romantic—or was it preplanned?—rendez-vous in Aspen last spring, and suddenly due to a snafu with the paperwork (where have we heard that before?) not only are Wyatt Lockhart and Adelaide Smythe still married, but thanks to the sparks that still exist between them, have given birth to twins.*

Now, trying to figure a way out of this mess, the lucky—or prodigiously unlucky!—couple has decided to move in together.

Once the legal issues are worked out, an amicable divorce is predicted to occur. That is, if a property settlement can be reached. Our legal experts tell us that ten years together makes nearly everything fair game financially for the ambitious new Lockhart Foundation CFO, and only daughter of criminal-at-large, Paul Smythe. A fact that should encourage rancher Wyatt Lockhart to firmly stake his claim on his kids and bide his time, exiting the precarious relationship...

"Lovely," Adelaide deadpanned, before she could stop herself. Even though neither she nor Wyatt had made a secret of their plans to become a family first, then consciously uncouple over the next year or so, it still stung to see it in print.

Hope frowned. "There are half a dozen more articles like this, and the news just got out a few days ago, when people started receiving their invitations to the party Lucille is giving on your behalf."

Wyatt narrowed his gaze. "I thought you said embracing the situation would lessen the scandal."

Hope smiled. "That's the good news. It probably has."

Adelaide sniffed miserably. "It doesn't feel that way."

"From a public-relations perspective, the real problem is Adelaide's father," Hope told them gently. "If Paul had been arrested and tried..."

"And were sitting in jail somewhere," Wyatt theorized, his need for justice as strong as ever.

"...the case closed," Hope continued, "then it would be old news. The fact he remains on the FBI's Most Wanted list keeps the story alive."

It was a good thing Wyatt didn't know someone was either contacting her on her dad's behalf, Adelaide thought with dread, or pretending to be Paul...

She swallowed. All the facts weren't in yet. There was no point in borrowing trouble. They had enough already. "So what should we do?"

she asked, wondering if this were going to impact her small salary as Lockhart Foundation CFO and the small accounting practice that kept her financially afloat.

"Well, you all know what I think," Lucille said.

"We're not staying married indefinitely, Mom," Wyatt warned.

Lucille wrung her hands. "But as long as you are, even for a little while, couldn't you just bow to public opinion, give this relationship your all and renew your vows to in some way lessen the talk?"

"No!" Wyatt and Adelaide said in unison. Thankfully, of one mind about that.

"We're not going to let our emotions—or anyone's else's—regarding our situation overrule common sense!" he insisted.

Adelaide agreed. "I've let myself be pushed into saying yes too many times in my life, when I really should have said no." She straightened to her full five feet seven inches. "This is one of those times."

"I agree." Wyatt wrapped his arm about her shoulders.

"It was just a suggestion," Lucille huffed, "but I still think you should keep in mind giving this marriage a real try."

"As much as I hate to differ with you, Lucille," Hope said, tactfully taking on her mother-in-law, "I would advise the opposite to curtail this kind of loose talk and speculation, if Wyatt and Adelaide are indeed still planning to divorce."

"We are," Wyatt and Adelaide said again in perfect unison.

Wyatt dropped his arm.

Hope accepted their decision in a way Wyatt's mom apparently could not. "The fact that the two of you have announced you intend to co-parent the children amicably and become a family is admirable. I haven't seen a single negative remark in print about that. But, the fact you've moved in together and everyone knows your marriage is still legal muddies the waters considerably. It's inviting speculation. Such as, how long will they actually all be under one roof? Will they or won't they stay married? Is it going to work out? If not, why not? In situations like this, rumors can go wild."

And with rumors came more embarrassment for Lucille and the rest of the Lockhart clan. "We really don't want that," Adelaide said quietly.

Hope understood. "Then, the sooner you wrap up all the legal details, as to the future plans of the two of you, and get those out there as a matter of public record, the better."

WYATT AND ADELAIDE called their respective attorneys and set up an appointment for the following afternoon, while Molly and Sage babysat the twins.

"We think it might be better if we go ahead and set our divorce in motion," Adelaide said, as she and Wyatt met with their lawyers in the conference room at Gannon's office.

Wyatt didn't know if it was the fact that the two of them hadn't made love again since learning of the new scandal, or just the fact they'd been really busy with the twins, but there was definitely renewed tension between him and Adelaide. He didn't like it. He also suspected it might disappear when they had the legalities wrapped up. At least for now. "So how long will it take?" he asked impatiently.

Claire McCabe explained, "Texas has a mandatory sixty-day waiting period. Which means the earliest the divorce can be granted is on the sixty-first day after the petition is filed."

Adelaide looked anything but relieved about that. "Does it ever take longer?" she asked.

"The average time is three to six months in an uncontested divorce," Gannon said.

Wyatt resisted the urge to reach over and take Adelaide's hand only because he sensed comfort was not what she wanted from him. "Is there anything prohibiting us from living together once the papers are filed? Like there was if we had wanted to go for an annulment?" he asked.

Gannon shook his head. "Not if it's an uncontested divorce."

Adelaide paled. "Can we pursue the dissolution in a way that doesn't assign fault to either of us?"

"Yes," Claire replied, "as long as you both swear under oath that the marriage can no longer continue because of differences that can't be resolved."

Gannon warned, "You will also have to agree on child support, visitation schedule and parenting times. Who gets the children on which holidays. And the division of any property."

Wyatt looked at Adelaide who seemed as overwhelmed as he was. She blew out a breath. "The property is easy enough."

Wyatt read her mind. "We'll both keep what's ours."

"As for the rest…" Adelaide relaxed slightly.

"Can't we just tell the court we'll decide on a day-to-day basis?"

Both lawyers shook their heads firmly. Claire said, "The court wants it all agreed upon—*in writing*—at the time the divorce petition is filed."

"And that's good for you all, too," Gannon chimed in, "since you will have a set of rules to follow if and when any disagreements do come up."

Which meant they couldn't go forward with anything until decisions were made. Wyatt swore silently.

Claire soothed, "We'll give you each work sheets to fill out. Take the time to think about what you each want. Then call us, and we'll all sit down together and hash out a final version that works for everyone."

"What are you thinking?" Wyatt asked when he and Adelaide left and headed toward the parking lot.

Her lips twisted ruefully. "That I don't think

I'll ever be able to split up our time with the kids the way it sounds like we're going to be required to do…at least on paper."

He followed her to his pickup truck. "Me, either."

Adelaide leaned against the side of the vehicle while he unlocked it and opened the door for her. "But, I see the point. It's not as if we intend to stay married."

He caught her hand before she could slip inside. "Do you want to date anyone?"

She gave him a shocked look. "What?"

"Do you want to date anyone else?"

"No." She sounded affronted. "Do you?"

"No." He flashed her a reckless grin, continued wryly, "So, that being the case, why do we have to divorce at all? Why not just stay legally married indefinitely, the way we first thought we would? Until we both feel the time is right for us to split up. Taking care of infants is a lot of work. Even with both of us, we're exhausted."

She clamped her arms in front of her, as if

warding off a sudden chill. "That's true." Worry clouded her eyes. "But there's still all the gossip to be quieted. Much as I'd like to just ignore it, we can't. We need to protect your mom and our families' reputations."

Wyatt studied her closely. "And that means no more scandal." He exhaled roughly. "The question is how? We can't do what my mother would prefer and recite vows we don't mean."

"I totally agree. We already did that once."

You *did that once*, Wyatt thought bitterly. *I meant mine then with all my heart and soul*. The question was, would he ever be able to mean them again if they did ever find themselves contemplating entering into a real marriage? Not just one that was continuing out of expedience.

"And we can't divorce." Oblivious to his thoughts, Adelaide rushed to add, "At least any time soon. So what do we do?"

Wyatt gave her a hand up as she climbed inside the cab. He watched her tug the hem of her skirt down to her knees. The glimpse of silky thigh filled his body with need. Deliberately, he pushed the desire away. "Let's talk to Hope. See if she has any more ideas."

Luckily, the crisis manager was available when they stopped by her office. "There must be another way that doesn't involve renewing our vows or getting a divorce," Adelaide said.

"Some middle ground," Wyatt persisted with a terse nod.

"Well, actually, there is one thing you can do." Hope rocked back in her desk chair. "You can always fight fire with fire."

Chapter Eight

"I can't believe we're doing this," Adelaide said the following morning.

Wyatt emerged from his pickup truck and walked around to open her door. He gave her a gentlemanly hand down, much as if they had been on a date. Leaning over, he brushed his lips across her temple. For show? Or for real? It was impossible to tell.

Straightening, he smiled down at her. Then promised, "It's just a few hours."

Adelaide shivered, whether from the wintry

February air or nerves, she did not know. "And a lot of scrutiny."

Wyatt wrapped a protective arm about her waist as he led her down Main Street toward his sister's coffee shop and bakery, The Cowgirl Chef.

"From afar." He leaned down to whisper in her ear, "Hope promised the paparazzo she hired to follow us around on our errands wouldn't get closer than a thousand feet."

Adelaide leaned into the curve of her husband's body, appreciating the warmth and strength. Her pulse pounding, she stopped to turn and look up at him. "Problem is, we don't know in which direction Marco Maletti will be shooting us from," she whispered.

Wyatt tucked a strand of hair behind her ear. "Like Hope said, it's best we don't know. Otherwise, it wouldn't look as if we were getting surreptitiously photographed. It's got to seem like these are unguarded moments."

When something was happening between them.

Something romantic, Hope had stressed.

Adelaide felt the heat pour into her face. "I don't know if I'm cut out for this," she confided in a trembling tone. She already felt ridiculously self-conscious.

He leaned down, and his lips brushed hers. "Then just don't think about it," he murmured huskily.

The next thing she knew, his arms were wrapped all the way around her, and his mouth was on hers. Hot and insistent. Patient and sweet. Caressing. Tempting. Her body responded with a tidal wave of lust.

Telling herself this was all for show and not what she really wanted deep down in her heart, Adelaide wrapped her arms about his neck and rose on tiptoe, pressing her body fully against the hardness of his. Avidly, she met his kiss.

And that was when they heard it.

Guffaws. Followed by a loud cough.

They broke apart and turned in time to see two of Wyatt's brothers, Chance and Garrett, grinning from ear to ear.

Both were in on Hope's plan to battle the rumors with an emerging "story" of their own. "Too bad Mom's not here to see this," Chance ribbed.

Garrett ran a hand along his jaw, teasing, "She'd think her fondest wish was coming true."

Lockhart family unity was also on Hope's agenda of things to be publicly demonstrated. Although in this case the action synched with Adelaide's instinct, too.

The members of the Lockhart clan were famously strong individually. United, they were invincible. It made her feel a lot safer, knowing that she and the twins were now part of the famous Texas family.

"Nice to see you." Adelaide went to give both big men a warm and welcoming hug. Like Wyatt, his brothers were tall and fit, with rangy muscular frames.

Chance winked. "Mom'd probably also tell you to get a room." Adelaide blushed, and they all laughed.

Garrett flashed a devilish smile. "Where are the little ones?"

Glad to have something else to focus on besides her PDA with their brother, Adelaide answered, "At the Circle H. Lucille and Hope are going to bring them into town in a little while."

Arm locked around her waist, Wyatt wheeled Adelaide in the direction of his sister's bistro. "Meantime, we've got a breakfast to get."

"Lots of luck." The brothers inclined their handsome heads down the street, where a line was coming out the door. "Sage has her usual crowd."

All of whom, as it turned out, wanted to congratulate Adelaide and Wyatt on their "news."

"Looks like love is in the air," the mayor said with a wink. "And it's not even Valentine's Day yet."

"Didn't the two of you elope on Valentine's Day?" his wife asked.

Wyatt grinned proudly. "Ten years ago."

"So you've got an anniversary coming up," Nurse Bess Monroe observed.

Her twin, Bridgett, winked. "The traditional gift is tin."

Family law attorney Liz Anderson said, "That's changed with the times. These days, the gift is supposed to be diamonds."

"I can't see Wyatt wearing diamonds," Rebecca Carrigan-McCabe said teasingly.

Octogenarian Tillie Cartwright squinted. "He'd look good in tin, though."

Chuckles abounded.

"Speaking of Valentine's Day, are the two of you volunteering for the Laramie Chili Festival?" the mayor asked.

It was a major fund-raiser for the community. As well as a good time.

"I'm manning the cutting-horse training demonstration at the fairgrounds," Wyatt said.

"Adelaide?"

"I'm on the planning committee for the Lockhart Foundation, and I also signed up for shifts in the LF Information booth as well as the WTWA Go Fishing game for children."

"She's also going to be assisting me," Wyatt added.

Adelaide whirled, a question in her eyes.

"Looks like it's news to your wife," Travis Anderson observed.

Adelaide batted her lashes comically. "I guess that must mean we are married."

Everyone laughed.

"Well, we're happy to have you both," the mayor said.

They chatted a little more, enjoying the warm congratulations from the community, then Wyatt and Adelaide walked out and headed across the street to the local park.

They sat side by side on a bench, munching on iced Danish pastry, stuffed with almonds, and made in the shape of bear claws. "You have to work today?" Wyatt asked.

"For about four hours this afternoon," Adelaide said, aware how cozy this all was.

"Can it be done at the ranch?"

"It's work for the foundation, so I need to do it at their office, on their computer system."

Which had state-of-the-art cybersecurity protection and more firewalls than anyone thought was necessary. But after the embezzlement scandal the previous summer, Adelaide wasn't about to take any chances. Or make it possible for her father, the foundation's previous CFO, to strike again.

Intuiting her need for comforting, Wyatt draped his arm along the back of the bench. "What about the twins?"

She snuggled against him, loving his warmth and his strength. "I've been taking them with me when I have to go in. There's usually no shortage of people willing to pitch in and hold Jake and Jenny if need be. Although most of the time they usually sleep. Probably because there actually *are* an abundant number of people willing and ready to hold them," she quipped. Unable to help herself, she scanned the surrounding landscaped areas. Saw nothing. No one. Which meant what? The paparazzo wasn't here yet, or he was? In any case, they wouldn't be able to spot him at that distance.

She turned back to Wyatt. Unlike her, he was totally relaxed and oblivious. "You?" she asked.

Playfully, he nudged his thigh against hers. "Troy and Flint can handle things at Wind River today."

"Do you have anything else you need to do today?"

He grinned sexily. "Just be with you."

That should have been comforting. Having him shadowing her. There to help with their twins while she recorded the latest donations, did the foundation payroll and updated the LF books. But right now all she could think about was her unoccupied home. Feeling more jittery than ever, Adelaide took another hasty sip of coffee, started to rise. "Listen, as long as we're in town, why don't we…?"

Firm hand on her shoulder, Wyatt tugged her

back down and delivered another long, toe-curling kiss.

Finding she was just as susceptible to his brazen seduction as ever, Adelaide drew back breathlessly. "What was that for?"

He waggled his brows. "In case Marco Maletti didn't get the last one."

"Is he here?"

Wyatt's eyes twinkled. "I assume so."

She let her gaze rove over his handsome face and powerfully built frame. "Meaning you haven't seen him?"

He looked at her, as if completely besotted. "Haven't really tried." He traced her lips with the pad of his thumb. Bent down to kiss her again. "I've been too busy looking at you."

"I really don't think…"

He captured her lips with his. When she could finally breathe again, Adelaide said, "You're enjoying this."

He caught her hand and held it over his heart. "Aren't you?"

"Heck, yes. But I'm not in the habit of making out in the middle of Laramie."

He tunneled his hands through the windswept strands of her hair, bent his head. And kissed her…cheek. "Maybe you should be." His lips ventured to the sensitive area just beneath her ear. As he worked his magic, it was all she could do not to moan out loud. There was absolutely nothing she could do about the dampness between her thighs.

Adelaide shut her eyes as another wave of desire sifted through her. Heaven help her. The reckless, wild boy—the one who had caused her so much trouble in her youth—was back.

"Your mother wouldn't approve," she argued weakly, sensing he was about to try to kiss her—really kiss her—again.

"Actually," Wyatt said with a grin, "I think she does."

Adelaide bolted upright. "What?"

He nodded. "She's over there, parked in front of the coffee shop. Waving. Looks like she was about to send Hope over to get us. To let us know the twins are here."

Was this Step 3 or 4 or 5 of their fight-fire-with-fire plan? Adelaide couldn't remember. She was so dazed from their smoldering hot make-out session.

She rose on wobbly legs. "Time to take them on a stroll?"

"Apparently so."

They walked across the street. A delighted Lucille approached them, just as the sun peeked through the clouds. "Everything's going well, I take it?"

"Oh, yes," Adelaide said. If you could discount how real it all felt, that was.

As Wyatt got the convertible double stroller out of the rear seat of his pickup truck, her phone went off.

She stepped back to answer it. Saw a Snap-chat had come in from someone she'd gone to college with.

Curious, she tapped on the icon and instantly

her screen was filled with a photo. Not of any of her pals, but of a deeply tanned fiftysomething man, with spiky peroxide bleached-yellow hair, a salt-and-pepper goatee, tropical shirt and cargo pants. He had a camera slung around his neck, earrings glinting from both ears. Sunglasses covered his eyes. She couldn't say how tall, but five feet ten inches seemed about right. He was a little chunky around the middle and had a gorgeous beach behind him. The message *Can't Wait To See You and the Kids!* flashed across the screen.

Causing Adelaide to take another, harder look.

Could that be…

My God.

Was that *her father*?

His nose was all wrong.

And he'd gained weight. Changed his hair.

But the rest of him…

The image disappeared. Meaning ten seconds had passed.

Wyatt and Lucille were both looking at her. "Is everything okay?" Lucille asked.

Adelaide thought about everything the matriarch and her entire family had already been through. Thanks to her criminal dad.

A chill went down her spine.

Ignoring the curiosity and concern in Wyatt's eyes, she forced a smile. "Yes. I just remembered something. Is it okay if I meet the two of you over at my house? I really need to check out the framing for the foundation of the new addition. See how that's going."

Without waiting for permission, tacit or otherwise, she rushed off.

"THIS WASN'T THE PLAN," Lucille said worriedly as Adelaide drove off in Wyatt's pickup truck, while he and his mom pushed the double stroller down Main Street. Wyatt knew that, and even worse, he sensed his wife was keeping something from him. *Again.* He hoped it was just about her house. Some unexpected—and probably costly—problem there she did not want to discuss.

He soothed his mother with a reassuring smile. "Adelaide and I can walk Jake and Jenny in her neighborhood, instead of the park, Mom. It will be fine." Which, as it happened, was only three blocks from historic downtown Laramie anyway.

Lucille fretted. "She looked white as a ghost to me."

To me, too, Wyatt thought. But there was no need to worry his mom. He pointed out casually, "Renovating can be nerve-racking, even when you have a normal amount of sleep."

His attempt to change the subject worked. "How are things going with the twins?" Lucille asked.

They make great chaperones. "We're still trying to get them on a schedule," he admitted.

"It'll happen. Although, in addition to the wind-up infant swings we brought you, you might try…" His mom proceeded to give him a dozen tips. Most of which went right in one ear and out the other because he was so focused on wondering what was going on with Adelaide.

Lucille squinted at him as they reached the front of Adelaide's home. Construction trucks were parked all around. "You think I'm interfering, don't you?"

I think you don't trust me to be as capable as my siblings would be in this situation. And we both know why.

But figuring it was best to let the ghosts of old problems recede into the past where they belonged, he said instead, "I think we're all doing our best, Mom, which is all we can do. Right?"

Lucille offered a smile so dubious it hurt. "Right."

Wyatt pushed aside his resentment. "Do you want to come inside?" he asked politely.

At the rear of the cottage, there was a lot of sawing and hammering going on. Lucille wheeled the stroller in the opposite direction. "I think I'll walk a little more. I don't want the construction noise to wake up our little darlings."

"Okay. I'll get Adelaide and be right out."

Familiar voices floated toward him as Wyatt walked in. Although the rear walls of her home were still intact, big drapes of heavy duty plastic had already been hung from ceiling to floor. Through the windows, Wyatt could see half a dozen workers putting together the frame for the addition to the cement foundation.

In the kitchen, his brother Chance and his wife, Molly, stood with Adelaide, who looked increasingly uneasy.

"So everything looked good to you, when you got here this morning?" Adelaide was asking.

The couple nodded. "Yeah. It was fine," Chance said.

Molly put her hand on Adelaide's shoulder. "Are you worried about your house being unoccupied?"

Adelaide hesitated as Wyatt closed the distance between them. "A little," she admitted as he took his place next to her.

"In a city as big as Dallas, that might be warranted," Molly soothed. "But here? No one is going to bother your stuff, Adelaide. Even if you left your door unlocked, it would still be fine."

Wyatt had the feeling that wasn't it. "Okay," Adelaide said.

"You ready to walk the twins?" he asked.

Behind him, more footsteps sounded. After a short rap at the door, Deputy Detective Kyle McCabe walked in.

ADELAIDE HAD ONLY to look at Wyatt's face to know he had completely misunderstood why the uniformed lawman was there. Figuring she'd know how to deal with that later, she smiled and said hello to their visitor, who also happened to be one of the first people she'd met in the community she now called home.

"Hey, Adelaide." Kyle gave her an affable hug, then turned to Wyatt. After the two men shook hands, Kyle continued, "I didn't know if you'd be by to check on the renovations today..."

He did however know about the creepy message she had just received, Adelaide thought. And—thanks to the surveillance software the department had installed on her phone—exactly where to find her. Not just now, but at all times.

"…but I'm glad I saw your vehicle because my parents tasked me with giving you a baby gift."

"That's sweet of them."

"They know how it is to deal with multiples…"

Adelaide chuckled. "I guess so, since they had five boys—triplets and twins!"

"Anyway, they thought whatever the gift is might help. So—" Kyle gave her a look that signaled he needed to speak with her privately "—it's out in the squad car."

"I can get it," Wyatt offered.

Guilt and anxiety flooded Adelaide. She had promised not to keep things from Wyatt but she had also privately vowed not to ever hurt him—or his family—unnecessarily again.

She would tell him everything—as soon as she could. Meantime, she would do what had to be done.

So, tensing with the duplicity required, Adelaide turned back to her husband. Aware it was all she could do not to wring her hands, said,

"Actually, would you mind going up the block and seeing if your mom needs some help? That double stroller can feel like a lot to push after a while."

Wyatt paused. Then met her gaze with a completely inscrutable one of his own. "Sure." He shook hands with Kyle again. "Nice to see you."

"Likewise."

While Wyatt headed off to catch up with his mom, who was almost to the next cross street, Adelaide walked out to the squad car with Kyle. The beautifully wrapped present was sitting on the front seat. "Is that a real gift or just a ploy to see me?"

"Both."

"You saw the photo-message on Snapchat?"

Kyle nodded imperceptibly. "Was it your dad?"

"I think so," Adelaide said nervously. "I mean his nose and his entire look were different, but yeah, I think so." It was an effort to stay casual. "Were you able to record the photo?"

"Yep." Kyle reached into the front seat and

got the package. "Have you told your husband what's been going on?"

Guilt flooded her anew. She and Wyatt had promised to be direct with each other...and here she was, already lying and hiding. "No."

"Good." Kyle handed the box to Adelaide. "Don't."

"He's going to get suspicious," Adelaide warned.

"The last thing we need is him interfering with our investigation by trying to protect you. You can tell him everything when it's all over." Kyle paused meaningfully. "But nothing, not a word, Adelaide, before then. I mean it."

Adelaide gulped nervously and nodded her head. She prayed this didn't backfire.

Chapter Nine

Hours later, Wyatt and Adelaide were back at the Wind River Ranch. Evening chores completed, Jenny and Jake asleep—at least for the time being—they finally had a chance to sit together on the sofa and open the gift from Annie and Travis McCabe.

Wyatt stared at the padded black cotton canvas garment with the thick straps and two open envelope-style pouches with holes along the bottom. "What is it?"

Adelaide's dark eyes dazzled with excitement. "A kangaroo-style carrier for twins."

"For one person?"

"And two babies. One in front, one in back."

He turned to face her, his knee nudging her thigh. "I didn't know they made those."

"I did." Adelaide's smile widened. "But it seemed impractical because I couldn't figure out how I was going to get both babies strapped in their compartments and then put it on by myself." She studied the accompanying literature, then leaped to her feet. "Mind if we try it on you?"

All for whatever made her happy, he said, "Sure."

She had to reach up to slip the contraption over his head. Her hair brushed against his chest and shoulder as she adjusted the length of the harness and fastened the clasps on either side of his waist.

It took a while.

He didn't mind.

She was gorgeous, with her delicate brow furrowed and her soft lips pursed in concentration.

Inhaling the sweet womanly scent of her, he stood, legs braced slightly apart, his arms akimbo as she walked around him, her hands sliding between the carrier and his body as she checked to make sure it was on securely.

"Now let's see if we can put something akin to two babies in it." She moved to the box of baby toys and returned with two stuffed teddy bears, one pink and one blue. "These are about the size of Jake and Jenny." She fit one in, facing his chest. Safety-strapped it in.

Then walked around behind him and did the same with the other.

Plucking the phone from her pocket, she opened it and stepped back. "Say cheese!"

He mugged at her comically. His pulse revved up even more as she sashayed back to him.

It had been several days since they'd had the opportunity and energy to make love, and he wanted her more than he had imagined possible.

Oblivious to the lusty direction of his thoughts, she beamed and held the photo out for him to see. "See how cool this is? We'll be able to carry both Jake and Jenny at one time, at least until their combined weight is thirty-five pounds."

Wyatt knew he would. He doubted Adelaide would be able to comfortably carry both for too much longer, given the way they were growing.

It was a good thing he was going to be around.

Adelaide picked up the note that had come with the present. She read it, then handed it over for him to peruse. "Annie and Travis McCabe said they used a similar one when Kyle and Kurt were infants, and they were still corralling their six-year-old triplets, Teddy, Tyler and Trevor. I'll have to call them in the morning and thank them."

Here was his chance to ask some of the questions that had been nagging at him all day. He wasn't normally a jealous guy. Maybe because he'd never had to compete for the attention of any woman he was interested in. But something about Kyle McCabe's visits, the past couple of days, didn't feel right to him.

It was almost as if he and Adelaide were hiding something.

What, he couldn't imagine.

"Why do you think Annie or Travis didn't stop by in person to deliver this to us? Their ranch is just five miles from here."

For a moment, she went very still.

"Do you think it's because you and Kyle are no longer dating? And Annie McCabe thought it might be awkward?"

Still wary, Adelaide lifted her chin. "I didn't know you were aware I dated Kyle when I first moved to Laramie."

For a moment, Wyatt let himself drown in the depths of her dark brown eyes. "Kyle McCabe is the only one of his brothers not married with kids."

She shrugged. "So?"

He inhaled the sweet smell of baby lotion clinging to her skin. "You were pregnant at the time, with no daddy in sight. Of course people took notice."

Just as he was now noticing Kyle's dual appearances.

She unhooked the belt buckles at his waist. Stepped back. He eased the carrier over his head and handed it to her. She turned and walked away, still not saying anything. He could practically see her emotional armor sliding back into place.

"Don't you have anything to add?" he asked quietly. The last thing he wanted was for them to go back to the anger and mistrust they'd experienced before they learned about the twins' parentage.

Whirling, a distant look came into her eyes. "I'm not sure what you want me to impart," she returned with unusual stoicism.

He couldn't shake the feeling she was protecting someone. "Was there a reason he stopped by in person a couple of days ago to ask you to do his tax return, and delivered the gift from his parents to you personally today?"

She stalked into the kitchen and stood on the

other side of the island, where they'd made love a few days before. "First of all, a lot of people have asked me to do their federal taxes for them. And I expect even more will before the April filing deadline. Second of all, he delivered the present to *us*."

Thanks to the tumultuous events in their past, Wyatt had a sixth sense when she was holding back from him. She was definitely doing so now. The force field around her heart had never been more fortified.

He had to find out why.

"So the fact the two of you stopped dating was mutual. Kyle's not interested in you romantically any longer?" he prodded.

To his frustration, her emotions became even more obscure. "We're…friends."

Who had spent at least ten minutes talking, their heads bent together, before Kyle left. Even half a block away, pushing a stroller, he had been able to see the subject matter had been both serious and intimate. "What's going on, Adelaide?"

he persisted. He knew there was something she was withholding.

Worse, she knew that he realized it.

And that knowledge broke the dam.

She threw up her hands. "Look, I know the whole hiring Marco Maletti plan was supposed to stay just within the Lockhart family, but I'm not so sure it's a good idea not to clue in at least someone in the sheriff's department."

Suddenly, her fierce defense and the defeated slump of her slender shoulders made sense. "So you went rogue on us and contacted Kyle?"

"No!" She circled around to stand in front of him again. "I had no idea Kyle was going to stop in when he did this morning. But then he was there, and he already knew stuff was going on…about us…"

"You mean he read the tabloid stories."

"He heard about them. Everyone in town has. They're just too polite to say anything to us about it directly."

"But Kyle did."

"No. But he—he wanted to know how I was, and so I just…I blurted it out. I told him in confidence that for the next few days or weeks we are going to be intermittently trailed and photographed by paparazzo Marco Maletti. And that it was with our permission, as part of a fight-fire-with-fire strategy. So that if someone saw something and reported it to the sheriff's department, Marco would not be arrested."

That certainly explained the ten-minute conversation with their heads bent together, Wyatt thought in relief.

Adelaide sighed. "And then I felt like maybe I shouldn't have told Kyle without first discussing the option with you-all. Which is what I should have done in the first place anyway."

He wrapped his arms around her waist. "Then why didn't you?"

She splayed her hands across his chest. "Because clearly I was the only one who thought keeping anything from local law enforcement was not a good idea."

He stroked his hand through her hair, pushing it away from her face. "So you went along to get along, the way you always do."

"Yes." Her chin trembled. "And then, because I didn't speak my mind," she admitted hoarsely, "I ended up getting myself in more trouble with you."

She bit her lip as her eyes searched his. "I know no one is supposed to know about our scandal-rebuttal plan but the Lockhart family. But, given how protective of their fellow citizens the residents of Laramie can be, I thought it was the right thing to do. For everyone."

Silence fell between them, followed by a wave of guilt.

Wyatt had to admit he hadn't given any thought to the jeopardy the freelance photographer Hope had hired could possibly be in.

He praised her foresight. "Sweetheart, I think it was a smart move. I'll let everyone else in the family know what you did, and why."

"And for the record? You have no reason to be jealous of Kyle McCabe."

The intensity in her low tone made him smile. "Is that so?"

"There was never any chemistry between us." She threw her arms about his neck and went up on tiptoe. Looking deep into his eyes, she whispered, "Not like what you and I have."

She pressed her lips to his, kissing him sweetly and evocatively. Each brush of her lips deeper and more intimate and searing than the last.

Though she had always been quick to respond, he had always been the one making the first move. It was a thrill to feel her melting against him helplessly, wanting him as much as he wanted her.

Resolved to cherish and care for her the way she deserved, he continued making out with her, slow dancing their way up the stairs to his king-size bed. In the glow of the moonlight pouring in through the windows, they faced each other once again.

He let her strip her sweater over her head and shimmy out of her jeans, just because it was so exciting to see her begin a striptease. But when it came to her bra and panties, it was all him.

When they were both naked once again, he kissed her long and hard and deep, until she made that low sound of acquiescence in the back of her throat.

Determined to make her his, he positioned himself between her legs, making lazy circles, moving up, in, until the moisture flowed. Eager to please her even more, he drew her onto the bed.

"MY TURN," SHE WHISPERED.

The silk of her hair sliding over him, she kissed and caressed her way down his large, muscular body, molding and exploring, erotically laying claim. Supplying him with everything that had been missing from his life.

Tenderness. Desire. The feeling of being not just wanted but needed.

Sensations ran riot through him. Taking him to the brink.

He found a condom.

She rolled it on.

Stretching over her, he slid his palms beneath her and lifted her in his arms. She arched against him, open and ready, and he slid into her, slowly pressing into her as deeply as he could go.

She was everything he had ever wanted.

Everything he needed. And more. And then there was no more thinking, only feeling, no more holding back, only hot, wet kisses and hotter pleasure.

She shuddered and cried out.

He caught the sound with his mouth, and then he too was catapulting into oblivion.

They held each other tight. Surrendering to whatever this was. Always had been. And always would be.

WYATT EASED AWAY from her, moving onto his side, drawing her into the warm inviting curve of his body. As she shifted to face him, pillowing her head on his broad shoulder, Adelaide buried her face in his chest. The comfort she should have felt after making love with Wyatt was only partially present. Undercut by the deep sense of guilt she felt.

They had promised they would be completely candid with each other this time. Stop holding back whatever was going on with each of them. So they could forge a better foundation for their family, whether they eventually divorced or not.

But she couldn't do that.

Not when it came to the situation with her dad. He was a criminal, and he was still at large. And apparently trying to contact her with an intent to see her and his grandchildren.

Which meant if her father wasn't back in Texas, he would be soon. A fact that could put them all in danger. Especially Wyatt, if he knew, because her husband would want to protect her and their babies, and personally bring her father to justice.

It wasn't necessary, given her ongoing, secret cooperation with authorities. She just wasn't sure Wyatt would accept that.

Or forgive her for holding back the truth now.

"What are you thinking about?" Wyatt rasped, pressing a kiss into her hair.

Adelaide sighed and cuddled closer. He felt so good. So big and strong and solid. Reassuring herself that the secrecy certainly would not be required for much longer—one way or another law enforcement would be able to solve the case—she snuggled even closer. "I was wondering if we had time to make love before the twins wake up again."

As if on cue, the baby monitor crackled. An indignant cry filtered through the air.

"Guess not." Wyatt chuckled ruefully.

Adelaide bussed his nose, teasing, "It's nothing that can't be picked up later." She grabbed her robe. "I better get there before Jenny wakes up Jake."

Wyatt tugged on his jeans. "You know it's her?"

Adelaide headed for the cribs. "Can't you tell their cries apart?"

"Not yet."

"You will." She scooped up Jenny. Miraculously, little Jake slept on.

"Maybe we should wake them both up," Wyatt suggested.

Adelaide shushed him with a finger pressed against his lips. "This way I only have to feed and change one at a time."

He caught her hand and kissed the back of it. "We," he corrected her, the light evocative caress reminding her of just what a tender and compelling lover he was. He followed her to the changing table. "And since I'm here, I think we should care for both now so we can all get the maximum amount of uninterrupted sleep later."

Adelaide studied him. Wyatt was right—she

was no longer a single parent. And although the day or night would come when he wasn't with her at times like these, right now, in this instance, he *was* here.

So she handed him Jenny to hold while she woke up their sleeping son. "You're right. Let's do this together."

Chapter Ten

The following morning, Wyatt again let his hired hands handle the horses and elected to instead help Adelaide with the twins. Who were both pretty darn fussy, Adelaide noted, after another only slightly less restless night.

A softly whimpering Jenny ensconced in his arms, Wyatt attempted to settle his big frame into the rocker-glider. Not an easy task. The chair that fit Adelaide's five-seven frame perfectly was at least 30 percent too small for him. Frowning, he shifted Jenny a little higher on his shoulder. "What we need is a man-size rocking chair."

No kidding. He looked like Papa Bear sitting in Mama Bear's chair.

Adelaide knelt and put Jake in the seat of the indoor baby swing. "Way ahead of you, cowboy," she said over her shoulder as she strapped the audibly complaining Jake into the seat, then cushioned him at the waist with rolled-up receiving blankets. Rising to her knees, she pushed the button on the top that would provide thirty minutes of gentle uninterrupted swinging back and forth.

Jake's expression turned from grouchy complaint to one of surprise as he began to move.

Back and forth. Back and forth.

Adelaide sat in front of her son, where he could see her. She smiled encouragingly.

He smiled back.

To Wyatt, she said, "I called the online baby superstore and express ordered their largest rocker-glider. It's supposed to be delivered here today. Once it arrives we'll be able to rock the kids at the same time."

Wyatt looked her over. "Will we have to stay in rhythm? Or be woefully out of synch, like old folks on the porch of the nursing home?"

Her heart pounding at the memories of when they'd last made love and the urgent need to do so again, Adelaide snickered. "Funny."

He waggled his brows in a way that let her know his thoughts were going in exactly the same direction. "Thanks."

Noting Jake had stopped fussing entirely, she said, "Want to try this with Jenny?"

"Sure." He rose and walked toward her.

Still on her knees, Adelaide moved the other baby swing right next to Jake's. With Wyatt's help, she situated Jenny, too.

Jenny's eyes widened in pleasant surprise as she began to swing.

A peaceful silence reigned. Wyatt extended a hand. "We're going to have to thank my mom for these."

Slanting him a curious glance, Adelaide rose. "So you admit Lucille really does know a thing or two about caring for children?"

He let go of her palm reluctantly. "Almost anyone would know more than me, but yeah, she was right about this."

And maybe other stuff, as well, Adelaide thought.

Like giving their marriage more of a chance than they had.

Pushing the unwanted notion away, she accompanied him to the kitchen. Adelaide brought the wheat flakes out of the pantry. Wyatt retrieved the milk and a pint of fresh blueberries. They fixed their bowls. "So how much do I owe you for the rocking chair?"

Surprised he would turn what had been a thoughtful gesture into a transaction, Adelaide hid her hurt with a smile. "Nothing." She took her breakfast and slid onto a stool at the counter. "It's a gift."

He lounged against the counter beside her,

bowl held against his chest. "A tenth-anniversary gift?"

"No," she said dryly, watching him eat with the same appetite he did everything else. "An 'I expect you to use it frequently to help us all out' kind of gift."

He poured more cereal into his bowl. "I think I can manage that."

"So what's your schedule like for the rest of the day?" Adelaide asked.

"Troy and Flint are taking care of the horses this morning, but I really want to work Durango myself once my mom and Sage get here."

Adelaide batted her lashes. "You don't want to spend two hours working on the menu for the Welcome to the Family party for the twins?"

He fed her the last blueberry from his bowl. "I think you know I might have five minutes of patience for that."

She fed him her last wheat flake. "I think you know that's about my limit, too."

He set their dishes aside, then pulled her into

his arms. "So why not let Sage and Mom baby-sit the twins and come with me?" He wrapped his arms about her waist. "You probably should ride the horse you're going to be using during the Chili Festival."

"I thought I was just going to be assisting you during the cutting-horse training demonstration at the fairgrounds."

"Like Vanna White?" He mimed the graceful movements of the TV game-show hostess.

Adelaide rolled her eyes. "I don't think an evening gown will work in the arena."

He rubbed his jaw. "You look mighty fetching in a pair of jeans and boots, though."

She blushed at his sexy once-over. "Seriously…"

"Seriously." Catching her hands once again, he reeled her in. "I'd really like you to join me out on the ranch this morning. It'll be good for both of us. Getting some fresh air." He pointed to the now happily snoozing twins in their matching baby swings. "And you know the Lockhart women can handle it."

Was this a date?

It felt like a date.

"Consider it our date morning," he drawled, reading her mind.

She hesitated.

"PG rated."

The twinkle in his eyes was irresistible. When was the last time she had played at anything? "All right," she agreed recklessly. "I confess… I'm dying to get back in the saddle again."

"Go get ready. I'll handle things down here."

By the time they had both dressed for the excursion, Sage, who had the morning off from her bistro, arrived. Once again, looking a little wan and definitely tired.

"Before you two head out to work with the horses, I have a favor to ask," Sage said. "You two really should have anything you want for the party."

"But?" Adelaide prodded.

Sage inhaled. "I'd really like it if you vetoed everything involving shrimp."

Adelaide was as shocked as Wyatt looked. It wasn't like his little sister to shy away from any ingredient. In fact, the cowgirl-chef liked to joke she could put a southwestern spin on any dish.

Sage held up a palm. "I got sick on it in early January, when I had that really awful stomach flu…and just the thought, the smell, anything to do with it. I can't…"

"Fine with me," Adelaide said cheerfully.

"Me, too," Wyatt agreed.

Sage sent them looks of gratitude and relief, just as a car engine sounded outside. Adelaide glanced out the window. "There's your mother now."

"So what do you know about Sage that I don't?" Wyatt asked after the preliminary menu had been approved—sans shrimp—and the two of them went out to the stables.

Oh, dear. She had been hoping he wouldn't ask. "Nothing," Adelaide fibbed.

Wyatt blocked her way to the tack room. "What do you intuit, then? 'Cause something is sure as hell going on."

Adelaide bit her lip. Reluctant to betray.

"Fine." He brushed by her, blanket and saddle in hand, and entered Buttercup's stall. "I'll ask Sage directly when we get back to the ranch house."

Adelaide watched him put on the halter, secure the reins. "No. Don't do that. I have a feeling your mom already suspects anyway."

Wyatt brushed past her and went back to the tack room. "Suspects what?"

Adelaide followed. "That Sage's life, like ours, is about to become a lot more complicated."

"How?" Wyatt carried the gear to Durango's stall. "She's not dating anyone." He sent Adelaide a sharp look over his shoulder. "She hasn't since she finally called it quits with TW and left Seattle for good."

"I know." Adelaide lingered in the aisle. "But

she's become really good friends with Nick Monroe since she moved to Laramie."

Wyatt adeptly saddled the big black gelding. Taking the reins, he led him out. "Isn't Nick intent on getting out of here?"

"Taking his family's Western-wear business public via venture-capital expansion? Yes."

Wyatt motioned for Adelaide to go into the courtyard, then paused at the next stall to get Buttercup, too. "So why would Sage get involved with him if he's leaving Laramie? Maybe even Texas altogether?"

Adelaide put her left foot in the stirrup, her hands on the horn, and swung herself up into the saddle. "I didn't say that she had."

Wyatt watched as she got settled, then handed her the reins. "But…?"

"Every time I go in The Cowgirl Chef, Nick's either just coming in for a quick cup of coffee or just leaving."

Wyatt moved lithely into the saddle. "So? Their businesses are both on Main Street." Bypassing the arena next to the barns and heading toward a pasture the size of a football field, he swung down to open a gate, then proceeded to hop back on his horse.

"It's more than that," Adelaide insisted. "She's close to him."

Wyatt frowned. "Hooking up close?"

Aware how good it felt to be out in the cold, crisp winter air, Adelaide shrugged. "I don't know exactly what's going on between them, Wyatt. Maybe Nick and Sage are just good friends, the way they keep telling everyone."

"And yet…?" he prodded.

"She seems different somehow and she's gained weight, despite having the stomach flu several times over the last few months. Then there's her new aversion to shrimp. When I was pregnant, I couldn't handle the smell of Swiss cheese for some reason. It just made me want to barf every single time. In fact, I still can't handle it."

Amusement flickered in his eyes. "I'll make an effort to keep it out of our fridge."

She returned his droll look. "Much appreciated."

Now if she could just keep him from breaking her heart again…

Where had that thought come from?

Misinterpreting her frown, Wyatt continued, "Back to Sage. If she is pregnant and is finally getting the baby she always wanted, why haven't she and Nick told anyone? I mean, he seems like the kind of guy who would step up whether it was planned or not."

Adelaide shrugged and adjusted her flat-brimmed hat against the late-morning sun. "Who knows? Maybe it isn't his. Maybe Nick doesn't know. Maybe it is their baby, and they just don't want to get married or do anything that would in any way complicate or interfere with his business plans right now." She sighed. "Or maybe she decided to have a family the way I thought I had, via artificial insemination, and then got involved with Nick…and now it's all too complicated to figure out."

Wyatt paused. "You really think Sage got inseminated, too?"

"All I can tell you is that last summer, when she and your mom and I were investigating the foundation scandal, and driving back and forth from Dallas to the ranch, we had a lot of time to talk about other stuff, too. I had just started my second trimester, and I was over the moon about finally becoming pregnant. Sage asked me a ton of questions about where I went and how it all worked, and confessed she had been thinking about going that route, too. Your mom blew up at her because she wanted Sage to find her own knight in shining armor and fall in love first, and then have kids."

Wyatt's gaze narrowed. "How did Sage react to that?"

"She just stopped talking about it. And your mother never mentioned it again, either. But if this is what Sage has done, then my sense is your mom is not going to take the news well. Especially if Sage is also falling for Nick. Because that would go back to your mother being right, that your sister should have waited."

Wyatt scowled, as fiercely protective of his family as ever. "Should I talk to Sage? Or Nick?"

"No! To both! And don't you dare tell Sage I suspect anything, either. This is her news to tell, in her own time. Assuming it's true. It might not be."

Wyatt directed his horse to do a right turn and motioned for Adelaide to do the same. "On the other hand, if Sage is pregnant, she can't hide it for long. So why doesn't she just tell Mom?"

"Probably because she's feeling hormonal and vulnerable and doesn't want this to become yet another family crisis." Adelaide brought her horse to a halt next to Wyatt's. "And she's probably right to protect Lucille, since we aren't out of the woods yet with our own Texas-size scandal. Speaking of which…" Adelaide scanned the countryside. "Do you think Marco Maletti is out there somewhere right now, taking photographs of us?"

"I can't spot him, but he's sure supposed to be."

Adelaide studied the vast acres of yellow winter grass, the strands of cedar and live oak. "I can't see anyone, either," she murmured, but she still couldn't shake the feeling that she was being constantly observed.

For reasons she didn't dare reveal.

Wyatt mistook the reason behind her unease. "Relax, sweetheart. This is going to be easy. Buttercup—the mare you're on—is fully trained as a cutting horse. Durango," he said, petting the two-year-old gelding's neck, "is still a work in progress, but he's coming along."

Happy to have something else to concentrate on, Adelaide held the reins and smiled. "What exactly are we going to do today?"

"First order of business is to take them straight and forward. Get them comfortable."

He waited until she drew up beside him, then

moved Durango, taking care to keep them at the same steady easy pace. "We're going to speed up just a bit," Wyatt explained. "And then slow down… A little more…"

Back and forth, they moved across the pasture. Their horses alert and eager to please.

Eventually, Wyatt led them to a small wooden bridge, where they worked on stepping up and down, and backing. Buttercup responded to the lightest touch of reins and leg. Durango was a little less sure of himself, but Wyatt was swift to offer gentle pats to the neck and murmurs of encouragement.

By the time their work session at the bridge was over, Durango was stopping and starting and moving over and around it with the same ease as Buttercup. Better yet, it was clear the horse not only trusted Wyatt to keep him out of trouble, he adored him.

"You're really good at this," Adelaide said, admiration in her tone.

Wyatt tipped his hat. "Why, thank you, Addie."

His eyes twinkled as they rode toward a stand of trees. "You're not so bad yourself."

"A little rusty." Especially at love. Not that her husband seemed to notice…

They stopped next to the pond, then dismounted to let their horses get a drink.

"How long since you've been on a horse?" Wyatt asked curiously.

Adelaide's inner thigh muscles were humming with the tension a long neglected workout brought. "A decade."

"You used to love to ride when we were kids," he recalled. It was how they had gotten close. Taking riding lessons every weekend. Later, when they'd both become old enough, they'd assisted with classes of younger kids. She'd focused on Western pleasure riding; Wyatt had taught cutting, reining and barrel racing. And competed in rodeo events, too.

Adelaide glanced at the wintry clouds, looming on the horizon. "After we broke up, I didn't want to go to the riding academy anymore."

He caught her gloved hand in his. "I figured you just changed your teaching times to avoid me."

Shrugging, she turned back to face him. Even through the leather, she could feel the warmth and strength of his fingers. A shiver of awareness swept through her. "No chance at all of us crossing paths if I didn't go there." She sighed and leaned back against the trunk of a live-oak tree. "It was bad enough seeing you at school." Every time she had seen him, it had felt as if her heart would shatter.

He lifted her hand and kissed the inside of her wrist. "Yeah, the end of our senior year pretty much sucked."

Adelaide let him put both arms around her. "Big time." They'd both skipped their prom and barely made appearances at post-graduation parties.

He smoothed the hair from her face. "I was surprised when you went into accounting. You'd always said you wanted to teach riding."

Adelaide rested both her hands on his chest. "I did."

"Then…?"

She breathed in the masculine fragrance unique to him. "There was a lot of pressure on me to follow in my dad's footsteps." She pushed back the ache of disappointment her father's crime had brought, and moved to get back on her horse. "It seemed like a way to get close to him, which was something I had always wanted."

Wyatt got back in the saddle, too. Reins in hand, he guided his horse through the beginning of another set of training exercises. "And did you?"

Adelaide followed his lead, taking Buttercup in a straight leisurely line, moving her mare's front end, then her rear. "Yes and no. I'm not sure anyone ever really knew my dad."

Wyatt worked Durango in a circle. "What do you mean?"

"He always resented the success of people like your parents. The hedge fund they built gave them wealth beyond their wildest dreams. My father felt he worked just as hard, managing the money, and doing the books for people like your folks. Yet, his net worth was so much less."

Wyatt pointed toward the windmill at the far end of the pasture. They rode off, side by side, adapting another easy, well-controlled pace. "Paul's resentment never showed."

"He had excellent social skills."

Wyatt slowed even more. When Durango showed fear and uncertainty as they neared the windmill, he guided his horse away in a smooth easy motion.

They rode a distance away, then turned and started back, this time from a wider, even easier vantage point. "Did you see what happened at the foundation coming?" Wyatt asked.

The unexpected question brought the heat of shame to her face. "No." With effort, she met Wyatt's searching gaze. "I was as shocked by the disappearance of the funds as everyone else. In fact, that's the real reason I headed up the initial forensic investigation for your mom. I was sure I'd exonerate my father."

His expression reflected his sympathy. "Only, you proved the opposite."

"And cleared everyone else at the foundation in the process." Adelaide paused. "It was important to me that no one but my dad and his mistress, Mirabelle Fanning, the bank VP who helped engineer the fraud on her end, were blamed."

Wyatt approached the windmill again. Durango got significantly closer, but when he tensed, he moved him away again. "Paul never explained anything to you?"

She sighed. Maybe it was good they were finally discussing this.

"No." Although Buttercup was showing no fear, Adelaide turned the mare away, too. Keeping pace, she continued, "It's probably good that my dad never hinted what he was up to, because if he had, I would have had to turn him in." Her heart clenched in her chest. "And what happened was hard enough as it was."

For once, Wyatt seemed to understand the depth of her loss. "I'm sorry your dad put you through that."

Adelaide's lower lip trembled. Without warning, her throat was clogged with tears. "I'm sorry he put us all through it."

Wyatt caught her reins and brought her and the mare in close. "It's all going to be okay, sweetheart," he reassured her.

And in that moment, Adelaide could *almost* believe it.

"HOW DID THE riding go?" Lucille asked when they walked back in several hours later.

Wyatt looked around, surprised at the difference a family could make. His ranch house had always been comfortable, but it had never been what anyone would call warm and cozy. Now, with Adelaide at his side, blushing prettily from the exertion of their afternoon, Jake and Jenny napping angelically in their travel cribs, his sister Sage in the kitchen, whipping up something that smelled delicious, and his mom in front of her laptop computer, still working on the details for the Welcome to the Family party for Adelaide and the twins, it was downright homey.

Who would have thought?

"Our session with the horses was great!" Adelaide went to the kitchen sink to wash up, her dark wavy hair tumbling about her face. "Wyatt got Durango to go all the way up to the windmill and stop. No problem."

Sage made a comical face. "And that's a plus because...?"

Wyatt had to admit, at the moment, Adelaide did sound like she had it bad. For him. A notion that made him grin.

Oblivious to the brother-sister teasing, Adelaide enthused, "A good cutting horse has to trust his rider, so he can go where he needs to go and do what he needs to do without even thinking about it. He's also really got to trust and like his trainer. And even though it's clear that unlike Buttercup—who's a cowgirl's dream—Durango is still a newbie at all this. I swear he would follow Wyatt anywhere."

Sage burst out laughing. "Maybe she should do your advertising."

Before he could stop himself, Wyatt said, "Or join me in the business."

At that, all three women blinked.

"Adelaide *has* a profession," Lucille said.

"But she's always wanted a career teaching riding," Wyatt informed her.

More stunned looks. "Is this true?" Sage asked.

"I thought you liked working at the Lockhart Foundation!" Lucille said, hurt.

In salvage mode, Adelaide swiftly lifted both hands, palms out. "I do."

"Then?" Lucille pressed, looking even more distressed.

"She would like working with me more," Wyatt insisted, matter-of-fact. Having just had a taste of how great life could be, if they just went back to a simpler time when they'd both been happy, before all the heartache and divisiveness of the last ten years, he turned to Adelaide. Who, to his surprise, was suddenly heading for her phone. Head down, gaze averted. He paused, wondering if he had gotten this all wrong. "Wouldn't you?"

"Doesn't matter," he thought he heard her mutter. She whirled back to face him and his family, the closeness they'd shared during their ride suddenly gone. Gaze serious, she said, "I think we've had enough changes."

An awkward silence fell.

Sage perked up. "Speaking of changes, have you seen the latest from the online gossip sites? The stuff that was posted late last night?"

Adelaide and Wyatt shook their heads.

Beaming, Lucille tapped on her keyboard. "I've got them bookmarked," she said, then proceeded to pull them up, one after the other.

The *Daily Texas Dish* featured a photo of Adelaide and Wyatt kissing outside Sage's bakery, his two older brothers looking on. It was next to another photo of Adelaide and Wyatt cooing over the twins in the stroller, on the sidewalk outside her home. The headline proclaimed: Infant Twins Have Made the Wyatt Lockhart–Adelaide Smythe Love Match a Family Affair!

Another from the *Dallas Morning Sun* gossip page showed Wyatt and Adelaide strolling hand in hand through the Laramie town park, sharing a sidelong glance. The caption proclaimed: As Valentine's Day Approaches, Is Love in the Air?

The third was on the website for *Personalities!* magazine. It showed Adelaide and Wyatt emerging from the bakery, under the banner: Secret Marriage Brings Peace to Texas Family Feud!

Appearing shaken, Adelaide moved uneasily onto a stool. "I can't believe we made a national magazine with this."

Deciding they both could use a drink after their rigorous outdoor activity, Wyatt went to fix two tall glasses of electrolyte-infused ice water.

"We made the national news with the embezzlement scandal at the foundation last summer," he reminded her.

"I much prefer these headlines," Lucille retorted happily, getting up to give Adelaide, then Wyatt, then Sage, all reassuring hugs. "And peace between our two families."

"It sure beats the stories that were out there a few days ago." Sage sighed.

Wyatt nodded. "We all owe Hope a debt of gratitude."

"And there were will be a fresh batch of photos posted tomorrow," Lucille added. "From the activities on the ranch today."

"Speaking of which," Adelaide cut in, "now that we've replaced the negative with the positive, do you think we can finally call off Marco Maletti and end the clandestine paparazzo-stalking?"

Chapter Eleven

"I'm all for ending the tabloid stuff, too," Wyatt admitted after his mother and sister had left.

With the twins still sleeping, he and Adelaide went up to change out of their horse-riding clothing and shower.

Not sure how much time they actually had, Adelaide stripped down to her skivvies. "Then why didn't you back me?"

Wyatt followed her into the master bathroom. "Because if Hope—a renowned crisis manager—says it's too soon to stop feeding positive stories and accompanying photos to the press, then it is." He pulled off his own shirt and jeans. Picking up his electric razor, he ran it over the stubble on his jaw. "Why does it bother you so much?" he asked.

Adelaide turned on the water in the shower, peeled off her undies and stepped into the masculine-tiled stall. She tipped her hair back, beneath the warm invigorating spray. "I don't like the idea of someone surreptitiously following us. Photographing…everything. It makes me feel vulnerable and exposed."

He opened the glass door and walked in, his gaze roving appreciately over her naked body. Taking her into his arms, he dropped hot, open-mouthed kisses along her jaw. "Like this…?"

A delicious shiver went through her. "Wyatt…"

He gripped her tighter, his mouth capturing hers. Lower still, she felt the force of his arousal, hot and demanding. A river of need swept through her. Hands sliding down her back to her hips, he urged her back against the wall and nudged her legs apart with his knee.

He kissed her again, one hand skimming a nipple, the other moving between her thighs. Drawing her into a sweet and pleasing current of desire, making her as wild for him as he was for her. Helplessly, she lifted herself against him. Wanting, needing. Trying to…then unable to… wait.

He held her until the aftershocks passed, then left her just long enough to roll on a condom. Stepping back into the shower, he lifted her so her legs were wrapped around his waist. Thrilled by the raw, primal need she saw on his face, she sank onto him, cresting together through wave after wave of seductive pleasure.

Wyatt knew Adelaide was wary of the future, as well as the here and now. He also knew this was the one thing—the only thing—that would make her feel better. And if it helped him, too, he thought as a sigh rippled through her, and then a moan, if it helped them get even closer, then so much the better.

He kissed her softly and tenderly, sliding into and out of her, possessing her rough and hard. Until she peaked again, exquisitely and erotically, and this time he came with her.

AFTERWARD, WITH THE babies still quiet, Adelaide wrapped herself in her cozy white terry-cloth robe. Emotions awhirl, she went to the suitcase containing her clothes.

He stopped drying his hair with a towel and ambled closer. "I can make room in my closet for you, you know."

His scent—all warm, sexy man—sent another thrill thrumming through her. "That's okay."

His smoky blue eyes leveled her. "Don't want to get too comfortable here?"

She rose, undergarments in hand, determined to be practical, even if he wouldn't be. "More like I don't want to overstep my bounds. Become even more intrusive to your living space than the twins and I already are."

"Hey." He caught her arm and reeled her back to his side. "Why so formal, sweetheart? I thought we had a good time this afternoon."

She smiled. "We did." Heaven help them, they did. In fact, if nothing stood in their way, they'd be making love again right now.

He let her go and rocked back on his heels, still searching her face. "Then…?" he prodded relentlessly.

"What? Are you sorry we made love again? Regretting we moved in together…?" His frown deepened in consternation.

Now he was definitely unhappy.

Adelaide swallowed. "No. Of course not. It's just…" Ignoring the way his gaze scanned the vee of her robe, she pulled the bodice modestly closer, angled her chin and tried again. "You and I have made a lot of changes really quickly."

In under two weeks, they had gone from finding out they were not actually divorced, to discovering *they* had twins, to moving in together, albeit temporarily.

"Because we had to," he countered, all implacable male. "What I want to know is why you're suddenly running so hot and cold again. Having fun with me, wanting to make love with me one minute, putting up all the barriers the next."

Exasperated, Adelaide ran her hands through her hair. "I'm unnerved because we're doing what we always do. Getting way, way ahead of ourselves!"

Wyatt gathered her in his arms. "No," he countered gruffly, "we're catching up."

Head lowering, he delivered another smoldering kiss.

"You see," she said breathlessly, throwing up her arms and pulling away. "There you go. Seducing me into being reckless again." *Making me feel really, truly married to you. Instead of in the process of consciously uncoupling.*

He shrugged affably. "What's wrong with that?"

Not about to reveal how vulnerable she felt, or how tempted she was to do as he had suggested earlier, and at least go back to teaching riding lessons part-time, while still continuing her work as CFO for the Lockhart Foundation, she folded her arms in front of her. "I like to think things through first." Not just react emotionally.

He dropped his towel and tugged on a pair of snug black boxer briefs. "Mulling over anything is overrated."

She tore her eyes from his lower half. "Says you."

He pulled a T-shirt over his head. "I like to go with my gut."

She turned away to slip on panties under her robe. "Well, when I go with my first instinct, and let myself be impulsive, I usually make the wrong decision." She slipped into the bathroom to put on her bra and camisole.

"Like...?"

Walking back out into the room, she looked him in the eye. "Agreeing to elope with you."

He sat on the edge of the bed. "Why did you do that, anyway? And then run away?"

Wyatt had never asked anything about that, never wanted to understand. From his vantage point, things were just the way they were. So Adelaide knew even wanting to talk about it was a big step for him. Just as her making love with him, after he had said they were either all in or all out of a physical relationship for the duration, was a big step for her.

So she took a leap of faith, too. She sat next to him on the edge of the bed, and told him what was in her heart, too. "I wanted to be with you, Wyatt. Really, really bad. I just wasn't ready for marriage when we set off for Vegas, and—" she was ashamed to say "—I knew it."

He craned his neck and asked softly, "Then why didn't you tell me that?"

"Because it was still what you wanted. And

what the reckless part of me wanted. But the more logical part knew it was a mistake."

"So you bolted."

They sat in tense silence.

Finally she looked into his eyes and asked the question that had haunted her. "Why were you so insistent we get married as soon as we both turned eighteen? Why were you in such a hurry for us both to grow up?"

"Because I didn't want the future my parents were trying to push on me. And the only time I felt good about myself, or really happy, was when I was with you."

Same here.

He grimaced, recalling that tumultuous time. "I was afraid if you went off to college, and I didn't, you would leave me behind."

"But you did go to A&M."

"Only for two years. And I pretty much flunked everything but the ranching and equestrian courses."

She waved off the defeat. "Only because you

weren't interested in the other stuff. You were bright enough to ace any course."

Falling silent, he pulled on the rest of his clothes.

"Is that why you spent your summers working rodeos as a pick-up rider?" she persisted, pulling on a pair of black yoga pants and a long-sleeved red T-shirt.

He gathered up their soiled riding clothes and tossed them into the hamper. "How do you know about that?"

"You and I might not have had a word to say to each other, and been very good at managing not to run into each other, but I knew what was going on with you. Through Sage and your mom."

His lips curved wryly. "They made sure I knew what was happening with you, too."

But had he been interested to hear? His expression gave no clue. Telling herself she had no reason to be disappointed if he hadn't been,

Adelaide grabbed the hamper of baby laundry. They headed downstairs.

While she added clothes to the washer, he lounged nearby. "Is my lack of college degree why you wouldn't want to go into business with me, teaching riding and training horses?" he asked as they entered the laundry area off the kitchen. "'Cause I thought we had a good time out there today. I thought you were finally having a taste of your dream career."

"Well, it's either that or your atrocious handwriting," she joked.

Not funny. Okay. Adelaide sobered. "You're right. I loved training the horses. But I can't make a life-altering decision like that on a whim. Because whenever I impulsively do something like deciding to buy the cottage in town..."

He picked up a stray bootie, their fingers brushing as he handed it to her. "Hey, that's a nice cozy house. Conveniently close to work, like you said."

Adelaide added soap and turned on the machine. "Yes, and I knew in the logical part of my brain that it was never going to be big enough for me and the twins unless I renovated it."

He shrugged. "You thought you could wait on that."

"And now that the twins are starting to sleep better because we figured out they need to be able to see each other to feel secure, I realize I could have waited a couple years to do the renovation, like I originally planned. But instead I was so anxious to get everything settled and comfy and right..."

Clearly intrigued, he met her gaze. "Just the way you are here?"

Back to that. "Keeping my clothes in a suitcase reminds me that this agreement we have to live together, for the sake of our kids, is only temporary."

And she needed to be reminded, lest she do something really foolish, like fall head over heels in love with him, all over again.

"What if it isn't?" Wyatt asked quietly, coming

closer yet. He cupped her face in his big hand. "What if you and I like being together, taking care of the kids together, making love together?" His voice dropped a husky notch. "What then?"

It would have been easy to say they should forget the divorce and stay together if it had been months, rather than mere days, that they had been bunking together.

But that simply wasn't the case.

Determined not to hurt him, Adelaide chose her words carefully. "It is great things are working out better than we could have envisioned at the outset."

He lifted a speculative brow. "But…?"

Trying not to think what his low, gruff voice did to rev up her insides, she said, "We're still in the honeymoon period. Immersed in the wonder of being together again in a way we never thought was going to be possible, and of having kids."

He slanted her an annoyed look. "You say that like it's a bad thing."

She lifted her palm. "I'm saying it's why we have to continue to be *cautious*. Whether we stay together as lovers for the long run is not as important as the fact that we're going to be the twins' parents for life." She paused to let her words sink in. "We have to make sure we can make that part of our relationship work ad infinitum before we even consider changing anything else."

"DON'T YOU LOOK like you just lost your best friend," Chance teased the following morning, when he and Molly dropped by Wind River with a basket of traditional German breakfast breads and cookies, three-year-old Braden in tow.

Braden frowned, looking around. "Where's the babies?" he asked, tipping his little cowboy hat back. "There's supposed to be babies! Two of 'em! A girl. And a boy!"

Molly elbowed Chance. "Told you we should have called first."

Chance elbowed the love of his life right

back. "Told you Wyatt might have said no to just dropping by."

"So where are they?" the little boy persisted.

"Adelaide had to go in to town to do some work at the foundation, so she took little Jake and Jenny with her."

Braden walked over to the baby swings. He pushed the buttons on top before anyone could stop him. The swings began moving back and forth. "Can I try?" He lifted a leg as if to climb in.

Chance hit the off buttons and quickly stopped the motion. "No, buddy, you're too big for these, but we can take you to ride the horses like we promised." He turned to Wyatt. "If that's still okay?"

Wyatt had given his bucking-bull-rancher brother and loved ones permission to ride on his property at any time.

"No problem."

Molly assessed Wyatt quietly. "Why don't you

two fellas head on out to the barn? I'll catch up with you in a minute."

"Sure thing." Chance shepherded the little boy out the back door.

Molly set her gift on the kitchen counter.

Wyatt tensed. "Something you want to talk to me about?"

"Yes, actually, there is."

ADELAIDE HAD JUST about wrapped up the accounting for both the Lockhart Foundation and the West Texas Warriors Assistance nonprofit, when Wyatt's sister-in-law, Hope, stuck her head in her office doorway.

Her hands hovering over the computer keyboard, she tensed. It wasn't unusual to see Hope there—not only was she married to the physician who ran both organizations, but she also handled the public relations for both organizations.

Still, Adelaide had to ask, "Everything okay with the twins?"

Hope waved off Adelaide's new mom tremors with a big grin. "Oh, yes. Currently, Lucille and Garrett are holding court with the rehabbing soldiers. My Max, no slouch, is doing the play by play. Which, due to the fact he's not quite one year old, amounts to a lot of clapping and laughing, and pointing and smiling. And the occasional 'dada,' 'nana,' and 'baby' thrown in for emphasis."

Adelaide rocked back in her chair. "I never have to worry about Jake and Jenny getting enough attention here."

"An understatement. Listen, Tank Dunlop's wife, Darcy, is here, and so are Sage and Molly—"

"I thought Lucille said that Molly, Chance and Braden went out to Wind River to ride today." Apparently Adelaide had just missed them.

"She did, but we had something come up this morning regarding the foundation's Chili Festival fund-raiser, so she left the guys there and came back into town to meet with us. Since you're on the steering committee, too, I was hoping you had time to join us in the conference room."

"Sure. Just let me shut everything down here and I'll be right in."

"So what's up?" Adelaide asked when she joined the group.

"The mayor called," Hope said. "Advance ticket sales have been through the roof. Nearly double what they were last year. So he's asking all the participants to make sure that they have enough to accommodate the extra crowds."

"So we want to know if we should either expand our Kids Go Fishing Family Fun booth to double the capacity," Molly said, "or add an additional activity geared for the four-to-ten-year-old set."

"We're going to need to order extra prizes, too," Sage said. "Although some of those could come from my bakery in the form of cookies or cake pops."

The group talked some more.

Adelaide ran the figures on cost. They looked

at their budget, the potential profits each idea could potentially make, and then decided to just have two go-fishing games, set up side by side.

Darcy agreed to line up additional ex-military and/or their spouses to supervise the activities. "So what are you getting each other for Valentine's Day?" Darcy asked as the meeting wound down.

Adelaide tensed at the thought of the traditionally romantic holiday.

"What my man always desires." Molly laughed. "More home-baked German pastries and cookies! In the shape of hearts, of course. Braden will help me make them."

Darcy turned to Hope. "Garrett and I arranged an overnight at a luxe hotel in Dallas—the weekend after. Max is going to stay with Lucille while we have our adults-only ooh-la-la!" Everyone laughed.

"Adelaide?" Darcy asked.

Oh, dear. Adelaide flushed. "Um...I don't know. Haven't even thought about it yet."

"Well, you should get him something," Sage, who was practically glowing with good health, said. "After all, it is your tenth wedding anniversary."

So everyone kept reminding them. Adelaide lobbed the ball right back into Sage's court. "Are you getting Nick Monroe something?"

"Actually, yeah." Squaring her shoulders, Sage beamed. "Since we're otherwise unattached, we agreed to give each other something jokey." She turned to Darcy, the only one of them who had been married to active duty military, and had to help her husband battle back from life-changing injuries. "What about you?"

Darcy radiated hard-won serenity. "Well, maybe it's because I nearly lost Tank when he was injured overseas. But I always make sure I give him something that lets him know I will always love him with all my heart. Because I never ever want him to feel taken for granted."

A collective "ahhh" filled the room.

A few tears were shed.

The women had just finished exchanging hugs all around, when a volunteer loomed in the doorway. "Adelaide? Kyle McCabe is here to see you."

"SORRY TO INTERRUPT," Kyle said when Adelaide met him in the hall. "But my twin brother, Kurt, has this baby buggy they used when his triplets were infants. It's been gathering dust. And he and Paige thought you might want to have it."

Adelaide smiled, hoping this was just a casual visit. And not anything related to her dad. "That sounds wonderful."

"It's in the back of my pickup truck now," Kyle continued, "if you want me to transfer it to your SUV."

Amused by how oblivious the single lawman seemed to the admiring female glances turned his way—what was it about a man in uniform?—Adelaide said, "Great. I'll walk out with you." She and Kyle took the elevator to the first floor, then walked through the lobby, past the glass-walled PT unit where rehabbing ex-military worked with physical therapists to re-gain their strength.

Kyle held the door for her and they strode side by side through the parking lot. As soon as they were out of earshot, Adelaide asked, under her breath, "Is this the only reason?" *Please say yes*.

He sobered. "No. Mirabelle Fanning was picked up yesterday with Interpol's help."

The hair on the back of Adelaide's neck stood up. "My dad?"

The deputy detective lowered the tailgate of his personal vehicle. "Still at large. Allegedly with most of the money they stole."

With effort, Adelaide kept her expression casual. "He left her?"

Kyle lifted out the collapsed buggy and set it on the ground. "Mirabelle Fanning says he was headed back to the States to see you and the twins."

The knowledge her dad might be coming to Texas hit her like a sucker punch to the gut. Not because she feared him harming them in any way; she knew he wouldn't. It was the thought of how Wyatt would take the news, and what that might do to their newly healing relationship, that scared her.

Kyle carried the collapsed buggy to the other end of the lot, where Adelaide's SUV was parked. "Has there been any other contact?"

"Aside from my phone and computer?"

He nodded. "Anything out of the ordinary?"

She pushed the button and watched the cargo door lift. "No."

Kyle moved a few things in order to set the collapsed buggy inside. He looked down at her genially. "You'll let me know if that changes."

Telling herself everything was going to be okay, Adelaide promised, just as cheerfully, "First thing."

In the meantime, they had another more immediate problem to solve.

WYATT PARKED AT the far end of the lot. Chance got out and removed Braden and his car seat.

They all watched Kyle try to put a huge collapsed pram into the back of Adelaide's SUV.

"Doesn't look like that's going to fit," Chance observed.

Especially with the twins' safety seats in the second row.

"Too big," three-year-old Braden pronounced solemnly.

Wyatt tried not to react to the sight of Adelaide with Kyle once again. To his knowledge, the two of them hadn't seen each other this much when they were dating. And why was the set of Adelaide's shoulders so tense while she was gazing up at the uniformed lawman?

Fighting back a worried frown, Wyatt said, "I'll see if they want to put in my truck."

"Hey, thanks for the horseback adventures and ride into town," Chance said.

"Yeah! Thanks, Uncle Wyatt!" Braden yelled.

"Anytime." Eager to see what was going on, Wyatt strode off.

Nearing the deputy detective's vehicle, he no-

ticed Adelaide was as white as a ghost. The usually affable Kyle was sober, too. The innate male
need to stake a claim on one's territory surfacing
quickly, Wyatt flashed a lazy grin. "Problem?"

Adelaide turned with a guilty start. "Yes," she
said, frustration and something else he couldn't
quite identify flashing in her dark eyes. Closing
the distance between them quickly, he wrapped
his arm around her shoulders for a hug hello.
"Kyle's brother and his wife, Paige, are lending
us a pram to use for the twins, but it won't fit in
my cargo area."

Noting Adelaide had not relaxed into his embrace the way she usually did, Wyatt let her go.
"No worries, sweetheart. It'll fit in my pickup."

"Problem solved." Abruptly, Kyle looked as
anxious to get out of there as Wyatt was to see
him go. Still, manners required a little more conversation. Wyatt extended his hand to the lawman. "That's really nice of your brother and his
wife."

"Yes." Adelaide reacted in kind. "Thank you

all so much!" She stepped forward to give Kyle the kind of casual southern hug that served as both goodbye and an expression of gratitude.

Wyatt had seen her make the gesture hundreds of times over the years, but this time, despite her aura of distraction, it seemed to carry the kind of emotional weight that made Wyatt feel he was still missing something.

Not love.

Not attraction.

But *something*...

Kyle tipped his hat. "You-all have a nice day." He ambled off.

Adelaide turned to Wyatt. "Do you want me to take this back inside the building and deal with it later, or put it in your truck now?"

"Let's do it now." He wanted a chance to talk to her and get a better handle on what was going on. "I think it will fit in the rear passenger compartment if I fold the seats."

Adelaide touched his arm as he picked up the pram. "I'll walk with you," she said quietly He nodded as they headed toward his truck. Maybe he was reading too much into the situation between Adelaide and Kyle. It was possible that because the two had briefly dated and then transitioned to friends, the situation between them was still awkward at times.

"Where are the twins?" he asked, folding the rear seats and setting the pram in his pickup.

"Inside with your mother and Garrett." She looked up at him and paused, her teeth raking across her lower lip. "Would you mind if we collected them and went back to the ranch now?"

Ignoring his instinct, which was to pull her all the way into his arms and hold her until her distress faded, he studied her instead. "And skip the grocery shopping and early dinner in town?"

She held his gaze, her expression pleading. "We can do both tomorrow. Can't we?"

He stroked a hand through her hair, then tucked a strand behind her ear. "Are you okay, Adelaide? You'd tell me if there was anything wrong, right?"

"Yes…of course." She drew a breath that lifted the swell of her breasts. "I'm just really ready to go home."

"Sure," he said, wrapping an arm around her. Maybe a night at Wind River was just what the four of them needed.

Chapter Twelve

"So this is 'tummy time,'" Wyatt observed later that same evening. They had spread blue and pink blankets in the middle of his king-size bed, and put the freshly bathed and pj'd twins on the center of each. Both were cooing as they waved their arms and kicked their feet. He and Adelaide stretched out beside the kids and kept them entertained, waving rattles and soft small stuffed toys in front of their faces.

Adelaide smiled with maternal tenderness as their babies played. "Well, it will be, as soon as we flip them over onto their tummies. First, I want them to get acclimated and know we are here to support them in their ongoing quest to be able to lift their little bodies up on their arms and look around."

"They certainly seem up for it tonight." Cheerful, not a fuss or complaint in sight.

The easy tenderness she bestowed on the twins was suddenly directed at him. "That's what an exhausting visit to town and a good nap will do."

He thought about the way she'd looked when she'd curled up on his sofa after they got home. Her dark hair spread out on the pillow, a soft knit blanket covering her abundant curves. Hours later, her cheeks still glowed a contented pink.

"For all of you?" he teased, watching her smile spread to her pretty dark brown eyes.

"Yes, well, sometimes new mommies need naps, too."

Noting Jake looked ready for a little more action, he asked, "Ready to do this?"

Nodding, she gently turned Jenny onto her tummy.

Wyatt followed suit with Jake.

Initially the twins seemed more befuddled than happy. Which was understandable, Wyatt thought. Babies weren't supposed to be put facedown unless they were supervised. "I think it might go better if they can see each other."

They positioned the twins so they were facing each other. For a moment, both babies lay with their heads to the sides, taking in their new position. Then Jake pushed himself up on his arms. Lifted his head. Saw his twin do the same. He grinned widely, gurgled. And fell back down, only to push up again.

Jenny mimicked her brother's actions, gurgling all the while.

Contentment drifted over them. "I can see why this would build strength," Wyatt said softly.

A connection, too.

Adelaide rested her head on her upraised hand and met his eyes. "This is how infants eventually learn to roll over. Get up off their tummies, onto all four limbs, then rock back and forth and crawl."

Wyatt tried to imagine that. Found he preferred just staying in the here and now. Things were so damn good. Surprisingly good…

Adelaide seemed to want to savor the moment, too. She watched the twins a few more minutes, her face suffused with pride. Then noted with amazement, "They're just *perfect*, aren't they?"

So far as we know. Wyatt tensed. Unable to help himself, he asked the question that had been nagging at him from the beginning. "But what if they're not?"

ADELAIDE BLINKED, not sure she followed. "What?"

"Perfect," Wyatt repeated soberly.

Adelaide rose to a sitting position. "But they are." How could he look at their children, with their gorgeous expressive faces and sturdy, healthy little bodies, their intent interest in the world around them, and think otherwise?

"They might not be." He gave her a hard look. "What if Jake turns out to have a learning disability? What if they both do?"

Okay, she could handle this. "Where is this coming from?" Adelaide asked calmly.

"I have the three Ds—dyslexia, dyscalculia and dysgraphia."

She shook her head. "That's not possible."

He just looked at her.

Adelaide's heart began to pound. "Wyatt, I went to school with you at Worthington Academy from second grade on. I think I would know if you'd had learning disabilities."

He exhaled roughly. "You would have if my parents hadn't employed expensive private tutors to teach me to read and if my parents hadn't convinced everyone that there was no need to put it on my records because it could be held against me in future endeavors. My grades were bad enough."

Adelaide defended him hotly, much as she had back then. "You were a C student because you didn't care, Wyatt. You didn't even finish the tests we took at school."

"Not because I didn't want to, but because I ran out of time. After a while," he said, puting his hand in front of little Jenny, and watching her latch on to his pinkie, "I adapted a who-gives-a-flying-squirrel attitude because it was easier. It made my lousy academic standing a badge of honor instead of a mark of shame."

Adelaide stretched out again and imitated Wyatt's move. "Did your siblings know?"

Little Jake latched on to her pinkie.

"Nope." Wyatt replaced his hand with a soft cloth rattle. "My parents knew my self-esteem was bad enough without adding fuel to the fire."

"Your sibs would have teased you?"

"We were *kids*. And growing up, as you probably recall, the four of us boys were rowdy as hell." His lips quirked. "Of course they would have teased me! And then suffered the consequences. But by then it wouldn't have mattered because the damage would have been done. So my parents never said anything to them, and I was grateful for it. 'Cause—" he jerked in a ragged breath and sat up "—I didn't want anyone to know, either."

Adelaide studied his stricken expression. Seeing the babies were beginning to tire, she turned them onto their backs and got the swaddling cloths. "You should have told me."

Wyatt scoffed. "Miss A-Plus Student? If you recall, you were always telling me to hit the books a little harder."

Her turn to feel stinging shame, Adelaide swallowed. "I'm sorry. I—"

"Don't be." He swaddled Jenny as well as she swaddled Jake. "As you can see, I succeeded despite everything." He leveled her with a glance. "I just want to know that if it does turn out that our kids have any similar deficit…" he said huskily.

"I—we—will find a way to help them overcome it, just as your parents did for you," Adelaide promised vehemently. She reached across the bed to clasp his hand. "But we won't keep it a secret. We'll make it a badge of honor, a symbol of raw courage and grace, from the get-go."

He squeezed her hand back, hard. Briefly they stood and embraced. Yet it still felt like so much was left unsaid, so Adelaide came back to him after they had put the sleepy twins to bed. His look said he knew she wanted to ask him something. Just wasn't sure how to do so.

"Yes…?" he prodded gently.

Adelaide got two beers out of the fridge. "Were the 'three Ds' the reason your mom has sort of always hovered over you a little more than your sibs?"

He added a hunk of sharp cheddar and a package of crackers. They carried their treat to the living room and settled on the sofa. With a fire burning cozily in the grate, the house quiet, it was the perfect time to talk. "In retrospect, I can see they were trying to protect me. To keep me from making the wrong decision and/or failing and being hurt, but it was their lack of faith in me that really stung."

Adelaide tipped her bottle to his. "Is this why you rely so heavily on your gut?"

"Yep." He savored the first taste of the golden brew. "I can't allow myself to overthink anything. Otherwise, I become paralyzed with the fear I'll let everyone close to me down."

She wished she could make every past hurt fade away. "I believe in you."

He returned her quiet glance with a wry smile. "One of the things I've always loved best about you."

Loved, Adelaide mused, as another silence fell. How she wished that were true, more desperately than she had realized. But she knew better than anyone that loving something about someone or even loving the way they could make you feel was not the same as being *in* love with him or her.

Yes, they got on well. Shared twins now. Made

spectacular love. But would that be enough? she worried. It was for now. But always…?

He misunderstood her silence. "It's okay, Adelaide," he said gruffly, setting aside their beverages and taking both her hands in his. "I never meant for this to be that big a deal with us. I just wanted you to know because of the pediatrician appointment coming up… I plan to ask the doctor about it. See at what point testing can be done."

"Except it's not okay, Wyatt." She leaned toward him. "It's still going on, isn't it? With your mom? It's the reason she sent you all those articles on being a good parent and husband straight off the bat."

"That—and she was matchmaking."

Adelaide shook her head. Wondering if Lucille knew how much her continued lack of faith was quietly devastating her son. "Because she didn't want you to blow it."

His brow lifted. An inscrutable expression crossed his face. "Am I?"

"No." She shifted over onto his lap, so she could wrap her arms around his shoulders. She buried her face in the comforting crook of his neck and hugged him tightly. "Not at all," she whispered in his ear.

"Good." He grinned. "Because that's the last thing I want."

His mouth came down on hers. Powerful. Evocative. She knew he needed to make love as much as she did. Needed the intense intimate connection that only the physical could bring.

Had they been in love again…

But they weren't.

Might never be.

She wasn't sure it was necessary, though, not when they had so much else going for them. The least of which was the children they adored.

Needing him naked, she unsnapped his shirt, tugged it off, then the T-shirt beneath. He paused to grin indulgently at her. "Taking the lead tonight, darlin'?"

"Appears so." She went to work on his jeans.

Tugged those off, too. Found a condom, rolled it on. "I need you inside me."

His eyes heated. "Inside you is good. Very good. And to that end…"

He drew her to her feet, stripped her bare, then sank on the sofa, pulling her back onto his lap. The insides of her thighs rubbed against the outside of his. The hardness of his erection teased the feminine heart of her. As he moved to push all the way inside, the burden she'd been carrying for what seemed forever began to fade. Guilt and regret replaced by raw, aching need. Something that went deeper than lust and was far more satisfying than simply sex.

Making love with him pulled at her heart and stirred all her senses. The clean musky scent of him, the smooth warm satin of his skin. The hardness of his muscles. The pulsing heat and force of his erection.

All combined with the tempting quest of his lips, the erotic sweep of his tongue, the all-encompassing way he could kiss her, until she was awash in pleasure.

Wyatt knew she'd reached out to him out of empathy and a need to comfort him. A better man would have rejected that. Not him. Not when he wanted her the way he did. In his house, with his kids, and with him. In bed and out, she was the best thing that had ever happened to him. And he wanted her to know it as he ran his hands over her supple curves and kissed her with an intensity that took their breath away. Whether or not she realized it, Adelaide had been his destiny, and she his, the first moment they'd met. He saw it in the way she'd always looked at him, like the sun rose and set in his eyes. He'd enjoyed it every time he made her laugh or smile. And felt it in every touch, every lingering caress.

Satisfaction unfurled within him as he turned her so they were stretched out, facing each other, her leg thrown across his hip. His own body quaking with the effort it took to suppress his own needs, he slid home once again. Gliding a hand between them, he caressed her gently, kissing her all the while, dragging his chest across her creamy breasts and rosy nipples, until her skin was so hot it burned and her hips rose instinctively to meet his, her open thighs rubbing with delicious friction against his. With a soft moan of delight, she kissed him with deep, urgent kisses that washed away all the heartache of the past and rocked his soul.

His own need spiraling, he shifted positions so she was beneath him. As he entered her again, she shuddered with pleasure and whimpered low in her throat, surrendering to him, to the two of them, as never before. He pinned her arms above her head, going slow and deep, until her body took up the same timeless rhythm as his, trembling and clenching around him. And then all was lost in the heat and tenderness that surrounded them.

THE NEXT DAY, while getting ready for the pediatrician appointment, Adelaide brought the conversation back to a topic he had hoped was closed. At least for now.

Adelaide packed the diaper bag. "I think you should tell your siblings. Not just because LDs can run in families…"

As he looked at his wife, Wyatt was almost sorry he let the information out. The empathy and compassion of the night before felt like pity this morning. Which was the hell of learning disabilities. He never knew if he was being over-sensitive, or suddenly just aware of how others saw him. Somehow deficient. Less than… In need of…

He forced himself to sound casual. "Been reading up on it?"

They eased the twins into their matching white fleece outerwear.

Adelaide's cheeks turned pink. "A little." She handed him the diaper bag, looped her shoulder bag over her arm. They scooped up the twins and carried them out to her SUV. The day was crisp and cold, but sunny. "I plan to do a lot more."

He liked the way she protected him. It felt right somehow. Always had. "You're a great wi—" He stopped at the frozen expression on her face. "Ah, friend," he corrected. "Anyone ever told you that?" He bent to make sure Jake was securely strapped in.

She did the same on the other side of the vehicle, for Jenny.

"Not the 'wife' part. But friend, yeah."

They straightened and climbed in. He returned her wry grin. "Sorry. I didn't want to offend you."

She watched him fit the key into the ignition. "You won't."

He liked the fact she let him drive. "I don't know." He gave her the slow, sexy once-over. "Some of those articles my mom sent me said some new moms can be pretty sensitive."

She snorted at his teasing. "I wouldn't worry about riling me up. But we do need to be concerned about being late to our appointment if we don't get a move on…"

Wyatt had planned to ask Adelaide what to expect as they drove into town. Unfortunately, she had a call from Molly and Chance regarding her renovation. There were several issues that needed discussion and resolution, and Adelaide spent the entire time working those out.

They arrived at the medical arts building and because they were the first appointment after lunch, were immediately ushered into an exam room by the nurse.

"So who have we here?" the nurse asked, looking at Wyatt.

"This is Jenny and Jake's daddy, Wyatt Lockhart."

"Right. I think I heard something about the two of you being married." Her glance went to their bare left hands. "Or, ah," she stammered, embarrassed to have possibly spoken out of turn.

"No. We are, actually," Adelaide said.

"And have been for the last ten years," Wyatt added.

The nurse shot him a look. "It's a long story," he said.

She looked torn between bemusement and concern. "I imagine so. Well, get the babies undressed down to their diapers. I'll be back in to weigh and measure them and then Dr. McCabe will be in."

"You said they have to get shots today?" Wyatt took his last chance to ask the questions he hadn't been able to voice earlier.

"Yes," Adelaide whispered back. "And let's not talk about it. I get nervous just thinking about it. And I don't want Jake and Jenny to feel my anxiety."

The odd thing was, Wyatt was beginning to feel a little worried about it, too. Which was weird, since he'd given plenty of shots to his horses. And never had a problem watching anyone else get an immunization, either.

Lacey McCabe breezed in. The mother of six grown daughters, the veteran pediatrician was known for her warmth and understanding. Which was why, Adelaide had explained to Wyatt the previous day, she had chosen Lacey as their babies' primary physician.

"So how is it going?" Lacey asked, checking the soft spots on Jake's head. She looked into his ears and eyes. "Get them on a schedule yet?"

"Sort of," Adelaide said.

Lacey examined the inside of Jake's mouth, then his skin. She paused to put a stethoscope in her ears, then bent to listen to Jake's heart and lungs. The little guy was so patient and cooperative, Wyatt couldn't help but be proud of him.

Lacey palpitated Jake's's abdomen, gently tested the movement of his hips and legs. Then undid the diaper and checked out that area, too. Finished, she handed Jake back to Wyatt and motioned for Adelaide to step forward and lay Jenny on the examining table, which she did. While the nurse took notes, Lacey began the same exam, all over again. "How long are they sleeping at night?" Lacey asked over her shoulder.

Adelaide smiled as Jenny cooed happily up at Lacey. "Four and a half hours straight if we're lucky. After that, they could wake up again anywhere from two to three hours."

Lacey grinned back at her small patient as she checked out her navel. "And how long are they awake then?"

Adelaide looked at Wyatt for confirmation. "Usually at least an hour. Sometimes two," he said. Liking the fact that Adelaide was giving him a chance to participate, too.

Lacey lifted Jenny off the table and gave her back to Adelaide. "Congratulations, Mom, Dad. Everything looks great on both of them. Now, what questions can I answer for you?"

While the nurse prepared the immunizations, Wyatt explained about his learning disabilities. Lacey listened intently. "LDs do run in families, but that doesn't mean your children will have them. We'll put notes in their charts, though, to be on the lookout. And if we find any deficiencies we'll get them the help they need immediately."

"Thanks," Wyatt said, feeling immensely relieved to have this out there.

"We appreciate that," Adelaide said.

"Anything else?" Lacey asked.

Adelaide and Wyatt exchanged glances and shook their heads.

Lacey went into efficiency mode. "Okay, we're going to get this next part over with as quickly as possible."

Thank heaven for that, Wyatt thought. He wasn't looking forward to the shots any more than Adelaide was.

"So what I'm going to do is have Daddy step outside with little Jake while we do Jenny's immunizations. And then we'll switch places, and have Mommy step outside with Jenny while Daddy comes back in with Jake."

The nurse opened the door. Just that quickly, Wyatt found himself out in the hall facing a collage of patient photos, all pinned to the middle of sunflowers. On the other side of the exam room door, he heard Lacey talking and Adelaide murmuring soothingly, followed by an indignant scream and hysterical crying.

Wyatt bit down on an oath. He couldn't even see anything and already empathetic tears were welling in his eyes. He was supposed to be the man here. His little guy was depending on him; they all were. Working to get it together, Wyatt blinked furiously as little Jake—who had no idea what was coming next—snuggled happily against his chest.

On the other side of the door, another indignant scream pierced the air, followed by more heartrending sobbing. Wyatt paced. Finally, for what seemed an eternity but in reality took only twenty seconds, the crying lessened and stopped.

The exam room door opened. Her eyes swimming with tears, Adelaide stepped out, comforting their little girl. Happy the traumatic episode was over, for Jenny anyway, Wyatt flashed

Adelaide a reassuring look, then followed Lacey into the exam room.

"Let's put Jake here." She pointed to one end of the cushioned table. "We don't want Jake to be able to push the syringe away, so you're going to have to gently hold his hands above his head. Yes, that's it. The first vaccination is oral, so we're going to slip it in and let Jake swallow it."

That was easy enough, Wyatt noted nervously, although his son didn't particularly seem to like the taste.

"Next we're going to have two injections. One on each thigh. We'll do them as quickly as we can." Lacey swabbed the area on Jake's upper left thigh, rubbing the area gently in preparation. "While you talk to him to distract him."

How had Adelaide managed this? His throat wouldn't even work! Lacey gave him a look, as if wondering if he was going to be able to man up. Wyatt found a surge of testosterone and smiled down at his son. "It's okay, buddy. It's all going to be over in a minute…" he soothed.

Lacey skillfully delivered the first injection.

Jake started in shock as the needle pierced his skin, grimaced, then drew in a breath and let out a cry even louder than his sister's. He was still sobbing like his little heart would break as the nurse moved in to put pressure on the wound and bandage the left thigh, while Lacey prepared, and administered, another shot into Jake's upper right leg. Jake—who had never stopped sobbing—wailed even more.

Lacey picked him up and handed him to Wyatt, tenderly giving little Jake's shoulder a final pat. "It's all over, little one," she promised. "Your daddy will make you feel all better."

And indeed, cuddled against Wyatt's chest, Jake had already stopped his sobbing. The nurse and doctor slipped out while Jake leaned back, staring up at Wyatt with wounded, tear-filled eyes. Seeming to say, *How could you have let that happen to me, Daddy? I thought you cared about me!*

And at that, Wyatt just lost it.

Adelaide came back in the room, her face damp. "Dr. McCabe said we can get them dressed now." She caught his gaze, and seeing his overflowing emotion, began to cry again.

So Wyatt did the only thing he could. He gathered her and Jenny into an embrace with him and little Jake. Together, the four of them took the time to pull themselves together.

"WELL, THAT WENT WELL, don't you think?" Adelaide quipped as the four of them finally made their way to her SUV, post-immunization instructions in hand.

Wyatt shook his head, knowing there was only one person in the world he could have let see him that vulnerable. Fortunately, she did not seem to think any less of him for his inability to man up there at the end. "I really did not think I was going to cry."

She poked fun at herself. "That's the difference between us. I *knew* I was going to lose it."

Aware he'd never felt more bonded to her and

the kids than he did at that moment, he fell into step beside her. Soberly, he reflected, "We're going to have to toughen up before the next round of immunizations, though. Because even if the twins don't recognize a syringe in two months, they certainly will after that." They didn't want their anxiety transferring to their kids, the way his parents' fear over his LDs had transferred to him.

"You're right." Adelaide's desire to be the best mom possible came into play. "They're going to rely on us to be strong and steady and calm. Not just for shots. But throat swabs. And procedures…"

Wyatt frowned, thinking about needles. "Stitches…"

She winced. "Don't even say that."

He shrugged, already trying to brace himself for the inevitable. "They're kids. Some stuff is bound to happen. Someone is going to fall off a bike, or out of a tree…"

"Oh my God. I remember when you broke your arm in third grade, playing Tarzan!"

"Tumble off a diving board at the pool…"

"That was Zane," Adelaide commiserated fondly. "Showing off."

"Or cut her hand in the kitchen," Wyatt recollected.

"Sage."

Wyatt paused next to the car and waited for the door to read the keypad signal and automatically unlock. "Even Garrett—" the oldest son who in many ways could do no wrong "—conked the back of his head when he was inner-tubing down the Guadalupe."

"And let's not forget Chance," Adelaide murmured as they both secured the kids into their safety seats. "Who actually did wreck his dirt bike and split open a knee." Straightening, she climbed into the front.

He leaned forward and briefly let his forehead rest against hers. "It's kind of a Lockhart family tradition."

"Not for me." Looking as if she were thinking about kissing him, Adelaide moved back and fit the end of her safety restraint into the clasp.

Aware this was not the time to start making out, he slanted her a glance. There was still a lot he didn't know about her childhood. Particularly, the years before they'd met. "You never got hurt?"

She shook her head. "I was far too cautious."

And in certain ways, Wyatt thought, she still was. Whether that worked to their advantage or disadvantage remained to be seen.

"I'M GLAD YOU were there with me today," Adelaide told Wyatt hours later, when the full effects of the twins' immunizations began to surface. "And I'm really glad you're here now." She would have hated to have to handle this alone, with both of the twins so fussy.

Looking more like a family man than ever, with little Jake clasped gently in his arms, Wyatt got out of his man-size rocking chair and walked over to hers. He leaned down so she could put a hand to Jake's too-rosy cheek. "What do you think? He feels really warm to me."

"To me, too." Adelaide shifted the child in her arms. "What do you think about Jenny?"

Wyatt touched her cheek with the back of his hand. He grimaced with worry. "She's warm, too."

Adelaide went in search of the infant first-aid kit. "Do you know how to take their temperatures?"

"Do I know!" Wyatt scoffed. At her skeptical look, he amended, "At least in theory."

She chuckled. What was it about men that made them reluctant to admit to any deficiencies? "Those articles your mother sent are coming in handy." At least the ones about being a daddy. She hadn't seen him reading up on being a husband. But then, she hadn't read anything about being a wife.

He watched her remove Jenny's diaper and put her across her lap. "We really have to do it rectally?" He watched her coat the thermometer with petroleum jelly.

"To get the best accuracy when they are this young. Which is yet another reason I'm glad you're here with me."

He mugged at her joke.

"It's 99.9," she read.

"One hundred," he declared.

Adelaide consulted the printout they'd gotten from the pediatrician. "We don't have to call the service if it's under 100.4."

"Good."

"It also says we can give them baths to bring their temps down and make them more comfortable."

Wyatt sat again, Jake and Jenny snuggled against his chest. He hummed as he rocked, and the twins quieted almost immediately.

Trying not to be distracted by the tender sight, Adelaide worked quickly to set up a bathing station on the kitchen island. "Good thing we have two baby bathtubs," Adelaide said, returning, and then reaching out to lift Jake out of Wyatt's arms.

He stood with Jenny. "Good thing we have a man-size rocking chair. I kept getting stuck in yours."

Adelaide laughed, aware that what could have turned into an extended time of misery and tears had instead turned into a sweet, joyous time she would always remember. Wishing Lucille could see Wyatt the way she did, and know just how wonderfully adept he was at nearly everything he'd tried, Adelaide kissed his jaw. "Have I told you yet what a great daddy you are?"

Grinning proudly, he leaned over to kiss her back. "In all the ways that count. Have I told you what a spectacular mommy you are?"

She nodded.

Now all they had to do was find a way to transfer the boundless love they felt for the kids to each other. And their family would be all set.

Chapter Thirteen

"You look amazingly cheerful for someone who's just spent the last forty-eight hours caring for babies with post-immunization fever and fussiness," Lucille remarked when she came by Friday morning to help Wyatt out with the twins while Adelaide ran errands in town.

"It's probably because I had such superior help from their daddy," Adelaide teased.

Well, that and the number of times she and Wyatt had also managed to make love, she added silently. Sweet and tender, hot and passionate, slow and sensual. Their sessions had run the gamut. Leaving them both relaxed and happy and feeling surprisingly closer. Almost as if they were in love.

Wyatt winked. "What can I tell you, Mom? All those how-to articles you sent me really did the trick."

"Something did." Lucille grinned approvingly at both of them. "How long do you think your errands will take, Adelaide?"

"Not sure. I'm going to—" *pick up the special-order Valentine's Day gift I got for Wyatt and* "—um, hit the grocery. The bank and the pharmacy. And I also want to check on the progress at my house."

"I told her to take her time. She deserves a morning to herself."

"I agree," Lucille said.

Adelaide went over to the wind-up swings, knelt and kissed each drowsy infant in turn. Wyatt was there to give her a gallant hand up, so she did what she never did, went with her gut and kissed him, too.

Maybe things would work out, she thought, better than they had ever dreamed.

"STEAK, POTATOES, SPINACH and cream. That looks like the makings of a man-pleasing meal if I ever saw one," Sage teased when she ran into Adelaide in the supermarket.

With the same needling affection, Adelaide checked out her sister-in-law's shopping basket. "Roast chicken and all the fixings." *Plus saltines, ginger ale.* "What might you be planning?"

Sage grinned. "Nick Monroe is coming over for a little early Valentine's Day dinner."

Adelaide hoped Sage didn't get her heart broken again. She deserved someone who would put her first, above all else. "Where's he going to be after that?"

"Sante Fe. Houston. Phoenix. Oklahoma City."

"So he really is trying to take Monroe's Western Wear national?"

"At least completely thoughout the southwestern United States."

Adelaide thought about how happy her friend appeared whenever Nick was around. "I'm sorry."

"It's good for him."

Adelaide said gently, "I meant for you."

Sage waved off her concern. "We talk all the time. That's not going to change. So. How are things with you and my big brother?"

"Good."

"I'm glad. I've never seen him this happy."

I've never been this happy. "Being blessed with twins—" and a daddy who doted on them as much as Wyatt did "—will do that for you."

"Mmm-hmm." Sage winked mischievously. "Plus a lot of other things."

"Speaking of which," Adelaide said, flashing a smile, "I've got to get back to the ranch."

"Okay. Give everyone my love. I'll see you at the Chili Festival."

Adelaide checked out, then wheeled her basket out to the lot. She had just finished putting her groceries inside, and shut the cargo door, when she caught sight of the bumper sticker on her SUV: Grandpa Can Fix Anything.

Grandpa? Her children had no grandfather. Wyatt's dad had passed, and hers was out of the country for good.

Wasn't he?

Hands shaking, she got in her car and immediately called Kyle McCabe. "I have no idea how it got there," she told the deputy detective.

"Did you have a bumper sticker prior to this?" he asked.

Adelaide's nerves jangled. "No."

"Is the bumper sticker magnetic?"

"Let me check." Adelaide got back out of her SUV. Phone to her ear, she touched the colorful slogan on the bumper. "Yes. It is. You can peel it on and off."

"Then it's probably the sticker that was stolen off a car parked at the community center a few days ago. We've had a rash of sticker thefts the last week or so. All are ending up on other cars. Who gets what seems to be pretty random. So you're probably the victim of a teenage prank, just meant to be a silly joke."

Relief flowed through her. "Oh, thank heaven. I thought…"

"Have you had any more contact from your father?"

"No. Nothing." Adelaide drew a deep breath. "Have you heard anything more?"

"Nope. The customs and immigration service and TSA have all been notified, but as I told you earlier, it's not likely he'd try to come into the country legally."

Adelaide tried to imagine her father catching a ride with a coyote who drove people across the border in the dead of night, swam the river or climbed a fence. All options seemed impossible. Which likely meant she was overreacting. "What should I do with the bumper sticker?"

"If you have time, it'd be great if you could drop it off at the station. You can just leave it at the front desk. They'll see it's returned to the original owner."

Glad nothing was happening to disrupt her life after all, Adelaide climbed back behind the wheel. "Thanks, Kyle."

"And Adelaide? If anything else seems out of the ordinary, don't hesitate to notify me."

"Thanks for coming over to help out today," Wyatt told his mom while they sat down to give the twins their midday feedings.

Lucille settled Jenny in her arms and offered her the bottle. "You know, you still have time to go out and get Adelaide something nice for Valentine's Day."

The assumption he was still a screwup stung. Wyatt threw a burp cloth over his shoulder. "You really think you have to micromanage me in the husband department?" He'd blown off the articles Lucille had sent on how to be a good spouse, but somehow, this was different. It harkened back to his childhood, when Lucille had felt the need to shadow only one of her children.

"You don't exactly have a normal marriage." She paused meaningfully. "A really nice gift might help."

So would a lack of maternal interference in his love life. "I've got it covered, Mom," he said gruffly. He had not only figured out what he was going to give Adelaide, he knew where he was going to get it and when he was going to gift it to her, too.

"That's good to hear."

Wyatt moved his son to his shoulder for a burp. "But there is something I'd like to discuss with you. Adelaide and I talked to the pediatrician about the possibility of the twins developing learning disabilities."

Lucille did the same with Jenny. "I know you told your brothers and sister about your dyslexia, dysgraphia and dyscalculia."

He studied the stiff set of his mother's lips. "You don't approve?"

Lucille sniffed. "I don't see it as necessary, especially now, with you doing so well. Your father and I went to a great deal of trouble to keep you from being adversely labeled."

When Jake burped, Wyatt offered him his bottle again. He slanted his mother a glance. Although she'd come over to care for the babies, she still wore a silk-wool sheath, cashmere cardigan and heels. "Why did you do that?"

"Having come from modest rural backgrounds, we knew what it was like to be discounted unfairly. We worried the same would happen to you, and we didn't want you to be denied any opportunities because of your learning disabilities. Especially when we had the means to see you overcame them, privately."

Wyatt sensed there was more. "And you and Dad didn't want it known, either."

Lucille cuddled Jenny lovingly. "The rich get extra scrutiny, Wyatt. If it had been publicly known, people would have said you didn't belong at Worthington Academy."

The premiere Dallas school for the elite. "Maybe because I didn't."

"You had so many accommodations there."

Silence fell.

"Do you know how many children with reading and writing and math challenges never graduate from high school, never mind go on to college?"

Wyatt tipped the bottle so Jake could get the last of the formula. "Too many. And the term is *learning disabled*, Mom. LDs are nothing to be embarrassed about. Nothing to hide."

"Your father and I worked very hard to protect you."

And she still was, even though he no longer needed it.

"I'm not going to apologize for that," Lucille continued stiffly.

Wyatt turned to see Adelaide standing in the doorway, groceries in her arms. His sister-in law, Hope, was right beside her. Clearly, they had both overheard. And wished they hadn't.

Adelaide walked in. "Sorry to interrupt, but Hope needs to talk to us."

The other woman shrugged out of her coat and plucked a computer tablet out of her bag. "Another story has surfaced in the tabloid press. We didn't plant it."

She brought it over for everyone to see.

The screen was filled with a series of grainy photographs of Adelaide and Kyle McCabe in his sheriff's department uniform. The two were standing outside the WTWA/Lockhart Foundation building in Laramie, talking intently. Another showed Kyle lifting the McCabe's baby pram out of his truck and showing Adelaide how it went from the collapsed state to a fully extended buggy, big enough for multiple infants. Another of Kyle and Adelaide smiling, hugging. Wyatt had been standing off to the side when that happened, but he'd been cut out of the picture. And later was shown standing alone.

The story beneath was both damning and salacious: *Smythe-Lockhart marriage already in trouble as Adelaide resumes love affair with legendary Texas lawman Kyle McCabe, leaving husband Wyatt Lockhart out in the cold.*

Reading it, Wyatt snorted.

Adelaide blushed in distress. "Obviously, this was taken the other day."

"But not by Marco Maletti," Hope said. "He wasn't even in Laramie. He was off in Houston, chasing another story."

Wyatt walked back and forth with Jake in his arms. He patted his son's back gently. "Then who…?"

"An amateur who asked to be paid via an online money service with a shady reputation. At least that's what my contact at the tabloid claims. It's why the photos are so bad. But you can see they are authentic because this actually happened. Kyle did stop by to see Adelaide when she was in town the other day."

"So we're being followed by another paparazzo?" Wyatt theorized grimly.

"Or a wannabe," Hope concluded. "All we know for certain is that this person wants the story to take a salacious turn."

Adelaide looked like she was going to cry. "Oh no."

"So now what?" Wyatt asked the highly efficient scandal manager.

Hope shut her tablet. "We stick to our plan. And keep feeding interesting, touchy-feely photos and positive stories to the tabloid press until interest fades."

"Has anyone told Kyle McCabe?" Adelaide asked grimly.

Hope shook her head. "Not that I know of. I was alerted because I follow these things as part of my job."

"I'll do it," Adelaide said. Before anyone else could offer, she grabbed her phone and stepped outside.

ADELAIDE CAME BACK IN, just as Hope and Lucille were leaving Wind River. "Talk to Kyle?" Wyatt asked.

She nodded tersely and walked over to the dual Pack 'N Plays. The twins were sound asleep. She stared down at their angelic faces, a faint smile on her face, admitting quietly, "He agreed with Hope, that it was likely the work of someone hoping to cash in or become part of the story, even vicariously."

He followed her into the kitchen. "Was that all he said?"

"Aside from the usual, if anyone bothers us, notify law enforcement? Yes." She took two thick hand-trimmed porterhouse steaks out of the package and put them into a glass baking dish. Then, turned to look at him, the walls going up around her heart as quickly and sturdily as ever. "Why?" she bit out.

Working to corral his disappointment, Wyatt came close enough to inhale her familiar womanly scent. "I'm just wondering why you stepped outside to make the call."

Her head bent over the task, Adelaide seasoned the steaks with a spicy dry rub. "Because I feel like this is my problem to solve," she retorted stubbornly.

Once again, she was pushing him away. "I disagree," he countered quietly.

Her slender form stiff with tension, Adelaide swung back to face him. "If it weren't for what my dad did, no one would give two spurs whether our two families get along or not. Yes, people who know us would be interested to find out we are married and have twins, but the news wouldn't be written up in the press. We wouldn't be forced to fight fire with fire and or have unknown paparazzo stalking us and anyone else who came into our path."

"Like Kyle McCabe."

Turbulent emotion filled her eyes. Her lower lip trembling, she admitted even more miserably, "Not to mention the fact that your entire family is now stuck doing damage control, right along with us!"

"They don't mind. I don't mind."

"Well, I do!" She threw up her hands in frustration. "I hate the fact that my family has caused your family so much pain!"

"What happened last summer at the foundation is over, Adelaide."

She sighed, closed her eyes, and shook her head. "Don't you see?" she whispered, rubbing her temples. "It'll never be over. Never!"

"Yes," he said firmly, "it will."

Unfortunately, she didn't seem to believe him.

Luckily, her guilt and remorse about the past were things he could ease. Closing the distance between them, he wrapped his arms around her waist.

"First of all, you're part of the Lockhart clan, too, now. And thanks to our marriage, have been for years. Even if we didn't know it." He buried his face in the fragrant softness of her hair, kissed her temple.

He paused to give her a long reassuring look. "Second, you don't need to handle any of this alone. Not anymore. Not even the apologies."

Adelaide gulped. Her eyes glistened moistly. "I was trying to protect you."

Her vulnerability broke his heart. Wanting to do everything and anything he could to ease her hurt, Wyatt brought her closer still. "I don't need your protection," he told her gruffly.

He was strong enough to shield all of them from whatever came their way. He threaded one hand through her hair, looked down at the fiercely loving expression on her face. "What I need…what I have always needed…and wanted, Addie…is just you."

Relief softened her slender frame. "Oh, Wyatt," she admitted softly, "I need and want you, too." She stroked her hands through his hair. "So much…"

He lowered his head, and kissed her passionately. To his delight, she kissed him right back, clinging to him with all she had, until all the walls she'd just erected came down, and the last of her inaccessibility faded.

Figuring it was time they took advantage of

the peaceful interlude, Wyatt caught her beneath her knees. "And now, as long as the twins are still sleeping," he teased, sweeping her gallantly up into his arms. He waggled his brows. "I have in mind something equally 'relaxing' we adults can do…"

She laughed shakily as he carried her up the stairs and dropped her down on the center of her queen-size bed.

"Mine?" she teased, knowing he liked space when he made love to her.

"This was closer," he told her gruffly. When she looked at him like that, all soft and sexy and needy, he couldn't wait any longer.

He stripped off her boots, jeans. Knelt on the bed to help her out of her pants, sweater and bra. She gasped as he kissed her again, ravenously, his hands discovering the deliciousness of her curves. Her nipples beading against the center of his palms, he moved lower. Past her navel. Lower still.

She arched as he caught the elastic edge of

her panties in his teeth and brought it down. In a shockingly short time he had her naked and crying out.

His own body thrumming with need, he stripped down, found a condom and joined her on the bed.

"Let me." Trembling, she rolled it on, then pushed him onto his back and swung her body lithely over his. Joyously, she moved to take him all the way inside. As their bodies merged, her eyes filled with an emotion that was as elusive as it was deep. The nameless ache within him spread, infiltrating his heart. Turning her, he moved over top of her, their mouths connecting as intimately as their bodies. Tongues twining, they kissed and kissed. His hands slid beneath her hips and he lifted her, going deeper, slower, then deeper again. With a soft, low groan, she rocked against him erotically, breathlessly. She shuddered in his arms. He plummeted right after her. They clung together, sharing the ecstasy, the peace.

Worried his weight might be too much for her, he rolled onto his back, taking her with him. Cuddling her close, he kissed her temple, ear, cheek. "For the record," he whispered, savoring the increasing intimacy between them, "I adore you, too."

ADELAIDE WOULD HAVE liked nothing more than to stay wrapped in his arms, their naked bodies entwined. But she had promised herself she was going to make him dinner. And with the twins newly asleep—five o'clock fast approaching— she needed to get started.

"Where are you going?" he asked huskily as she eased out of his arms.

Damned if the sight of him, sprawled naked in her bed, wasn't the most beautiful sight she had ever seen. She pulled on her panties and secured her bra. with him watching lustily all the while.

"I got steaks. Remember?"

When she bent to pick up her pants, a small velvet jeweler's box tumbled out onto the floor.

He lifted a brow. "What have we here?"

Maybe there would be less pressure if she gave it to him now.

"Your Valentine's Day gift." She sat on the edge of the bed, pretending a casual ease she couldn't begin to feel. She searched his eyes. "Want to open it now?"

"It's February 12. I haven't had time to pick up your gift yet."

"So we'll draw out the pleasure."

His big body relaxed. "Well, now I'm curious."

"It's also sort of a fun anniversary gift," she added nervously as he took the gift box. She hoped she hadn't overstepped. "Practical, too. In the sense that maybe if we use them, we'll get less questions at places like the pediatrician's office. At least for the time being."

His brow lifted.

Adelaide drew a breath. "I'll be quiet now."

Grinning sexily, he opened the lid. Looked inside at the two identical twisted tin-and-sterling-silver tenth anniversary rings that could easily double as wedding bands.

One for her.

One for him.

There was a moment when he didn't move. At all. A moment where she wished they had never made a promise to consciously uncouple and then split up when the twins were older and the time was right.

But they had.

And with the secret she was still keeping from him, her father still on the loose, maybe even edging closer right this very second, she couldn't ask him to put a halt on any divorce plans and really try to make their marriage work.

Then he looked up at her, his eyes dark with desire, and something else she couldn't identify.

Something he, too, seemed reluctant to suggest, for fear it would somehow jinx the closeness they were already feeling, with every moment that passed.

"It's just for now," she said hastily.

"For appearances," he confirmed, his expression even more tender, yet inscrutable.

"And fun." And love… Because she was falling in love with him, all over again. And unless she was mistaken, he was beginning to want much more from her than they'd already agreed upon, too…

"This," he said gruffly, as he slipped the larger band on his left hand, then put hers on her ring finger, "is a gift as perfect as you."

There was only one problem with that, she thought, as Wyatt laid her down and made sweet and tender love to her all over again.

They had a lot going for them. *A lot*. But she wasn't perfect. Not even close. Or she wouldn't still be forced to keep so much from him.

Chapter Fourteen

"We may have a lead on the photo of you and Kyle McCabe," Hope told Adelaide early Saturday morning as they worked to set up the go-fishing games at the Chili Festival.

Darcy lined up the troughs. "Tank told me that the guys at the WTWA have seen a guy who could be military veteran who might need help but is not yet ready to ask."

Sage followed behind, filling the receptacles with water and plastic sea life. "I saw him, too."

Adelaide tensed. "What did he look like?"

Sage grimaced as a cook-off participant went by with a great big bowl of freshly sliced onions. "I couldn't see much of his face. He had on dark glasses and a hat pulled low over his eyes. But he had a kind of mangy-looking beard. Long salt-and-pepper hair in a braid that just reached his shoulders. I hate to say it, but he sort of looked— and smelled—homeless."

That didn't seem like her dad. He had always been meticulously dressed and groomed. Then again, the last photo she had seen of Paul had been as a beach bum. Could this be another disguise? Or someone else? "Was he dressed in camouflage?"

"No." Sage unrolled the banner for the front of their fund-raising booth. "He wore faded jeans, a flannel shirt, an olive-green sweater and a really filthy shearling coat. Military-issue boots, bedroll and backpack, though."

Sage straightened and massaged her lower back. "Nick said he went into Monroe's and paid cash for some new wool hiking socks, and a couple of boxes of trail mix and protein bars."

Molly turned to Darcy. "So why would anyone think he was the person who sent the photo to the tabloid?"

"'Cause he was carrying a cell phone," she replied. "Tank said he always seems to have it out."

"And while he was in the store with Nick, some of the customers were talking about all the paparazzo photos that had just appeared online, and they were speculating how much you could get paid for something like that," Sage added.

Hope, who had been busy unpacking boxes, began setting up a second row of troughs. "It could have been one of the locals, then."

"Except for one thing," Darcy stated, adding more fish toys to the water. "The people of Laramie County take care of their own. I mean, they'll all *talk* about what's going on until the cows come home, but selling you out would go against the grain."

Adelaide tried not to be paranoid. It wasn't easy given the messages, the apprehension of her father's accomplice, Mirabelle Fanning, and the bumper sticker that had appeared on her car while she was grocery shopping.

Plus, she couldn't shake the feeling she was being followed. Although that was probably Marco Maletti, who was supposed to be surreptitiously taking more photos of them to generate positive press.

Adelaide paused to appreciate the smell of spicy chili, funnel cakes and corn dogs scenting the air. "When's the last time anyone saw this guy?"

"A couple days ago," Darcy said. She waved over a vendor and purchased a hot cup of coffee for everyone but Sage, who declined the offer. "When you were at the Lockhart Foundation, getting caught up on the books. And speaking of catching up on things," Darcy said, pausing as she was in the act of handing over a disposable cup, "what do we have here on your left hand?"

Sage gasped. "Is that a wedding ring?"

Hope squinted. "Looks more like a roll of barbed wire molded into a band to me. What kind of metal is that?"

Adelaide fought back a self-conscious blush. "It's a mixture of twisted tin and sterling silver. I got them for us for a combination ten-year anniversary and Valentine's Day gift."

Smiles all around. "What did he give you?" Molly teased.

Adelaide released a dreamy sigh. "Don't know. He's making me wait until this evening."

"Ahhh," everyone said in unison.

Wyatt walked along the midway. Catching them looking his way, he waved. "He looks so cute with Jenny and Jake in that kangaroo-pouch twin carrier."

He sure did. Wyatt had foregone his usual Stetson, and his wheat-colored hair shone gold in the morning sunshine. To better accommodate the twins, he'd swapped out his usual denim jacket for a black fleece. The soft warm fabric molded his broad chest and provided a cozy resting place for the faces of their two twins, who were both busy snuggling against their daddy and looking around.

As their eyes caught, Adelaide and Wyatt exchanged smiles before he got waylaid again by another couple wanting to gush over the twins. "He's on daddy detail this morning. Lucille is going to have them this afternoon while Wyatt and I do the cutting-horse training demonstration. And we'll both have them this evening."

"Sounds like things are looking up," Hope said encouragingly.

They were. Adelaide just hoped nothing happened to mess it up.

"Oh, no." Darcy looked around, then, through the empty boxes. "The gates are supposed to open any minute now, and I forgot to bring the boxes of prizes!"

"Where are they?" Adelaide asked.

"They're in the white West Texas Warrior Assistance van. I parked it in the lot about ten rows back from the gate. They're in the cargo area. They have WTWA written in red on them. And there's a dolly there, too."

"I'll run and get them. You keep working on this."

Darcy handed over the key. "You sure you don't mind?"

Adelaide winked and shook her head. "The exercise will do me good." She also needed to clear her head. All morning long she kept having this foreboding that all her worlds were about to collide, and it was ridiculous. Nothing bad was going to happen today.

Still, halfway there, she had the unsettling sensation she was being followed. She turned, saw nothing out of the ordinary, just festival-goers and volunteers moving through the parking lot to the gates of the fairgrounds.

With a deep breath, she shook it off and kept going.

She had just located the WTWA van when a man fitting the description of the homeless veteran stepped out in front of her, the intent expression on his weather-beaten face telling her their meeting was no accident. Her stomach roiled with nerves. "Can I help you?"

"Actually, Adelaide," he returned with surprising confidence, "it's more what I can do for you."

THE PERSON IN front of her was a stranger. Unrecognizable. But she would know that voice anywhere. This was her secret wish and worst nightmare all rolled into one.

"Dad?" she asked hoarsely. He'd been a touristy beach bum in the last photo she'd seen. Now he was a down-on-his-luck ex-soldier, allegedly returning to his cowboy roots.

The man the world had once known as successful CFO Paul Smythe tipped his hat but kept a casual distance. His weathered lips formed an affectionate smile. "You look good, Adelaide."

Still reeling from the shock, her knees began to wobble. Her dad looked so much older beneath the beard and long scraggly salt-and-pepper hair. As if whatever high he'd experienced after getting away with a fortune had faded fast.

"What are you doing here?" Adelaide demanded, still not quite believing her eyes. What was he thinking, returning to Laramie? Near the family he'd stolen from, of all places…!

Was he *trying* to get caught?

"I want to make amends." Paul shook his head, his lips pursing in regret. "I should never have left you, honey."

He was right; he shouldn't have. Adelaide swallowed around the increasing tightness of her throat. The tears she had long refused to let fall flooded her eyes, blurring her vision. "But you did run away with Mirabelle Fanning, Dad," she reminded him bitterly, unable to contain her hurt a second longer. "Without so much as a note, or a goodbye."

Paul set down his backpack and bedroll, leaning it on the car parked next to the WTWA van. "That was a mistake," he admitted as festival-goers several rows over headed excitedly for the fairgrounds entrance. "*She* was a mistake. And it's over."

Joy mingled with distrust. "You broke up?" She noted her father did not seem to know his former paramour had been arrested.

Her dad's jaw set. "I found out Mirabelle was going to leave me for a much younger man last November, so I bolted first, with all the remaining cash."

"And it was after that you put the remote log-in on my computer and started contacting me through social media."

He pushed the sunglasses higher on the bridge of his newly reconstructed nose. "I couldn't say much. But I wanted you to know I still cared about you. I love you, Adelaide. I know I wasn't very good about showing it in the past, but that's going to change. We have a chance to be the family we always should have been. You, me, the twins."

Finally her dad was saying the words she had

always wanted to hear. And yet, they rang hollow. Her palms dampening, she said, "I can't leave Wyatt, Dad. I can't take his kids from him." *And I can't run off with an embezzler.*

Paul picked up his backpack and bedroll, and stomped closer, "Listen to me, honey. I know what it's like to be won over by a pretty face, but the *only* reason that reckless cowboy is back with you is because of the twins. And that's only temporary. The first time you disappoint him or he gets a little jealous—"

Everything clicked into place. "*You* sent the photo of me and Kyle McCabe to the tabloids!"

Her father acknowledged it with a lift of his brow. "I wanted you to see Wyatt's true colors. Put the real side of him, the ugly side, out there."

The only person who was being ugly here, Adelaide couldn't help but think, was her father. "Your ploy didn't work, Dad. Wyatt didn't jump to conclusions and think I was unfaithful with Kyle, or blame me for the additional bad publicity."

Paul scoffed and shook his head in mute remonstration. "Then it will be something else he won't be able to forgive. In the end, the result will be the same. You'll disappoint Wyatt—just the way you always have."

Adelaide really wished that weren't true. Deep down, she worried it might be. Because she always had eventually let down Wyatt in the past. To the point that if, it weren't for the twins, they wouldn't be together now.

"And when that happens, honey, he'll walk away. But this time he won't just break your heart, he and his family will take your kids, Adelaide. Just the way they took the money I should have had all along from me!"

Adelaide had always known her father could hold a grudge. She had just never imagined he would take one this far. "So the embezzlement was some sort of payback," she theorized quietly.

Just as she'd feared.

"Frank Lockhart and I built that hedge fund

together. I was on board from the very first, but he's the one who walked away with five hundred million dollars in the end, while I cashed out with less than twenty-five million."

Adelaide was familiar enough with the company's books to understand why that had been the case. "Frank and Lucille took really big risks with their money. They gambled big and won big. You were a lot more fiscally conservative. And I get that. In your place, with a wife and child to be responsible for, no other land or money to fall back on, I would have been really cautious, too."

Her dad scowled. "Not in the end, I wasn't. I bet it all and walked away with half their remaining assets."

It hadn't been just the late Frank Lockhart and his wife, Lucille, who Paul had stolen from. "You bankrupted their charitable foundation."

Paul's jaw set. "I took what was mine. Now you need to do the same, Adelaide."

"I can't."

Paul hardened his stance. "You'll regret it if you don't."

What she was regretting was this conversation.

"Because sooner or later—probably sooner—you and Wyatt are going to have problems," her dad said knowingly. "And when that happens, you'll find yourself on the losing end of one heck of a custody fight."

"Wyatt would never try to take the kids from me."

Paul snorted. "If you think he'll let you have the kids, even half-time, you're fooling yourself. Wyatt is an all-or-nothing kind of guy who, like the rest of the Lockharts, will stop at nothing to get what he wants."

He paused to let his words sink in. "They're used to having it all. They won't rest until they have your kids, too."

Much as Adelaide wanted to discount everything her father said, the insecure part of her could not do that. Because he was right. Garrett had wanted Hope—against all odds, he'd made her his wife and adopted her son. Chance had enjoyed similar success with Molly and her son, Braden. Lucille wanted she and Wyatt to make theirs a real marriage, instead of a pathway to an amicable divorce, and was pulling out all the stops to facilitate that, too. And though the Wyatt she loved now would never try to deprive her of their twins, even if the two of them couldn't get along long-term, the Wyatt who had refused to forgive her before might...

"This is our second chance, Adelaide," her dad cajoled softly. "The only chance I'll have to get to know my grandkids."

She knew that, too. And as much as she wanted to reconcile with her father, to be able to forgive him so she wouldn't have to spend the rest of her life hurt and angry, it wasn't that simple. "I can't go on the run, Dad. I can't have the twins constantly needing to change their identity, the way you have, just to avoid detection."

"You won't have to. I've got it all worked out. New identities for all of you, with accompanying ID and fake passports. Transportation into Canada, and from there to a beautiful chalet in Switzerland. All you have to do," he coaxed, "is meet me at four o'clock tomorrow morning, and you and the twins will spend the rest of your lives in unbelievable luxury, same as me."

"THAT WAS SOME FESTIVAL," Wyatt said hours later as he and Adelaide carried the sleeping twins into Wind River and up the stairs to the nursery. They'd stayed at the festival long enough to enjoy some of the prize-winning chili, and enjoy a little dancing, before heading back to the ranch.

She met his gaze, overwhelming emotion and something akin to gratitude glittering in her dark brown eyes. "Really wonderful," she whispered back.

Carefully, they placed Jake and Jenny into their cribs and eased off their winter caps and fleece outerwear.

Wyatt paused to admire their beautiful children, then took Adelaide's hand and led her back down the stairs. She seemed curiously over-wrought and on edge. "Want a glass of wine?"

She shook her head. "It would make me too sleepy. The twins will be awake again for feed-ing at 2:00 a.m."

Aware it was a little chilly in the house, he cranked up the heat. "Are you okay, sweet-heart?"

She stared at him with an expression of calm indifference. "What do you mean?"

He watched her narrow her eyes. "You've been in a weird mood all day."

She paused, as if searching for a way to ex-plain. "It was just a really long day."

Wyatt knew that.

"With a lot of confusion."

He knelt to light a fire, then stood and faced her. "You're kind of used to both, now that we have twins," he teased gently, sauntering closer. "Aren't you?"

She ran her hands through her hair, lifting the

wavy mass away from her scalp. "Today was a whole other kind of stress."

"Is that why you slipped away a couple of times?"

Her hands stilled. "What are you talking about?"

"Sage said it took you forever to come back with the prizes for the go-fishing games. They were about to send out a search party for you."

She dropped her arms to her sides. "I got way-laid in the parking lot. Talking."

"And then this afternoon." Taking her by the hand, he reeled her into his side. "You were almost late for the cutting-horse demonstration. And no one could find you."

She turned bright pink and pulled away. Walking into the kitchen, she got herself a glass of water. "The lines were so long for the ladies' rooms, I thought it would be faster to use the gas station half a mile down the road from the fairgrounds."

He watched her make up a few more bottles of formula for the twins. "You drove there?"

She flushed all the more, shrugged. "Sometimes you just got to do what you have to do." She gave him a terse look that warned him not to pursue it.

He got the hint. Moved on, waiting until she had finished, then gently gathered her in his arms. "We still have time for my Valentine's Day anniversary gift to you."

She stiffened and pulled away. Switching off the lights in the kitchen, she returned to the hearth. "I'd rather not do that tonight."

She had to be kidding, right? He drew her into his arms once again. This time she did not pull away. "How come?"

Sighing, she said, "I think we'll both enjoy it more tomorrow evening. When we're not so tired."

She had a point. Now that he looked closely, he could see she seemed completely exhausted, emotionally and otherwise. Yet curiously wired, too. "You want to go to bed now?"

Maybe a little lovemaking and a night of snuggling was just what they needed. He kissed her neck, the sensitive spot just behind her ear. "I think I could handle that."

She splayed her hands across his chest. Clearly as averse to the idea as he was for it. "I meant separately." The walls were right back up again. "You in your bed, me in mine."

He narrowed his eyes at her. Now she was really freaking him out. "You haven't done that since you got here."

She nodded, determination radiated in her gaze. "I feel like I'm going to be restless, and I'd rather not have to worry about keeping you awake." Her voice dropped an urgent notch. "Please tell me you're okay with that."

Was this some sort of test? he wondered, bewildered. It seemed to be. If she wanted proof of the depth of his feelings, he would give it to her. "Okay," he conceded softly. "But first I want a good-night kiss." His lips claimed hers, drinking in the sweet essence of her mouth. He expected her to melt against him, really get into it, the way she always did. Instead, she kissed him back with uncommon reserve, her body drawn as tight as a guitar string.

Surprised, he ran a hand down her spine. "You really are tense, Adelaide."

"I know." She dropped her head and let it rest against his chest. "I'm sorry." She released a shaky breath, even as her fingers gripped the fabric of his shirt before flattening and smoothing outward across his pecs. Sorrow and regret were reflected in her eyes. "Forgive me?"

What could he say? She had asked for so little. Given so much. "Of course."

Her slender body relaxing with relief, she headed up the stairs.

TWENTY MINUTES LATER, they were both in their beds, on opposite sides of the loft-like second floor of the converted barn, the twins sleeping soundly in their cribs.

As Adelaide had predicted, she was restless.

Tossing and turning every few minutes in the moonlit darkness.

Frustration roiled through him. He wanted to go to her, convince her to come to bed with him, work his magic on her to alleviate her stress. However, she had asked for her space, and he was honor-bound to give it to her.

But still it took everything he had not to demand answers. Mostly because he knew something was bothering her, and had been for days now. What exactly, he didn't know.

In the past he would have immediately assumed it was because he was failing to meet her expectations on some level and let her withdraw without ever telling him why.

Now he wanted to know so he could fix it.

Because only then would he be able to make his move and suggest they reevaluate their initial plan to consciously uncouple.

Meantime, he needed to get some sleep, too. So that tomorrow, when Adelaide wasn't exhausted from the long day at the Chili Festival and caring for the twins, they'd be able to enjoy the romantic late evening he had planned. And celebrate a belated Valentine's Day and tenth anniversary.

At 2:00 a.m. the twins woke. Wyatt got up to help Adelaide change and feed them before putting their exhausted little ones back to bed.

This time she did climb into bed and wrap her arms around him. He fell asleep, with her snuggled up against his chest. Only to wake two hours later to an empty bed beside him and the sound of a door downstairs softly closing.

He sat bolt upright. "Adelaide?" he called out softly.

No response.

Wary of waking the twins, he threw back the covers and padded barefoot across the top floor. His wife was nowhere in sight.

He went downstairs.

It was dark there, too.

Adelaide's coat, bag and keys were gone.

He moved to the front window. Saw her moving stealthily in the moonlight, the kangaroo-style twin baby carrier looped over her shoulders.

Swearing, he dashed back up the stairs to the cribs.

The twins were there, still sleeping soundly, their little chests rising and falling with every gentle breath they took.

So what was in the twin baby carrier?

Why was Adelaide wearing it?

And why, he wondered, as he moved to the window and saw her walking deliberately down the lane that led to the highway, a flashlight shining the way in front of her, was she going off in the middle of the night alone? Could she be sleepwalking? Attempting to meet someone? Maybe someone who was blackmailing her with other photos that could further embarrass his family?

All Wyatt knew for certain was that every instinct he had told him Adelaide was in danger.

Much as he wanted to run off after her, he couldn't leave their children behind unattended.

Nor could he take them with him, without possibly putting them in jeopardy. So he did the only thing he knew to do. Called for reinforcements.

The Laramie County Sheriff's Department emergency operator patched him right through.

To Kyle McCabe.

"Stay where you are." The deputy detective ordered gruffly. "Don't turn on any lights. Inside or out. And don't call anyone else."

Wyatt was transferred back to the emergency operator. "What the hell's going on?"

No sooner were the words out of his mouth than a car drove along the highway to the entrance of the ranch. Stopped. The door opened, the interior lights of the car illuminating a figure getting out. And then all hell broke loose.

HALF A DOZEN patrol cars and what looked like an arrest later, Adelaide was escorted safely back to the house by another officer. Rio Vasquez walked a pale, shaken Adelaide inside. "She's going to need to come down to the station later to make a statement, but right now, she should just stay put. Get some rest."

Rio thanked her again for all her help, then exited.

Trembling, Adelaide slipped off the baby carrier and sat on the sofa. Her coat still on, she removed the stuffed animals from the twin pouches, set them aside with a sigh.

He waited.

She said nothing.

Now that the danger was over, his temper rose. "I'm pretty sure I'm due some sort of explanation."

Her shoulders slumped in defeat. "My father just got arrested." The rest of the story came tumbling out.

He listened in disbelief. "So all this time, since the twins were born, you knew this could happen. Paul could show up!"

She looked at him, her gaze wary. "I knew it was possible, but I didn't think my dad would be that foolish. He's never been imprudent. Well, until he stole the money from the foundation. That was pretty crazy."

"Not to mention criminal."

A tense silence fell.

Once again, she appeared to bear the weight of what her father had done.

Guilt and compassion tempered his mood. Working to control his anger, he sat down beside her and took her hands in his. "Okay. I get why you helped law enforcement. I'm glad you did." He paused to control his mounting emotions. "I just don't understand why you didn't tell me! Let me know that you and our kids could be in danger! Especially after our agreement not to lie to each other or keep things from each other from here on out. So we wouldn't end up in situations like this!"

Adelaide pulled free, stood and walked away. She glared at him with weary resentment. "I was instructed not to inform you." Belatedly, she shrugged out of her coat.

So what? "I'm your husband," he reminded her angrily. "Or doesn't that count for anything?"

"Of course it counts, Wyatt!" Her motions stiff and mechanical, she walked over to hang it up. "But law enforcement didn't want you involved."

She, either, apparently.

He strode closer. "Why in blazes not, since this is my family we're talking about!"

He met her gaze, surprised to find her eyes shiny with tears and regret.

"Because they know how reckless you can be. They didn't want you going off half-cocked, looking for my dad and trying to bring him in by yourself! Or doing anything else that would screw up their investigation and arrest."

He forced himself to calm down. "Okay. That explains them. It doesn't explain you." He corralled his hurt. "Why you didn't tell me in confidence?"

"I already told you!" She threw up her hands in exasperation. "I was following the orders I was given."

Grimly, he shook his head. "It's more than that and we both know it."

She clamped her arms beneath her breasts. "Like what?"

Disappointment churned in his gut. "You haven't trusted me in the past. You clearly don't trust me now," he accused bitterly.

She took a step back. Her eyes glittered moistly. "You're wrong, Wyatt," she said in a low, choked voice. "I do trust you."

"So why didn't you think I had a right to know?" he demanded furiously, refusing to let her run away. "Why didn't you insist the sheriff's department fill me in, too?"

She threw up her hands in frustration. "Because I didn't want to argue with them about the proper way to proceed."

That he could buy. Jaw set, he looked her in the eye, and demanded, "Then why didn't you tell me privately? We're not just legally married, Addie, we're in a committed relationship." Or at least he'd thought they were! "You could have claimed spousal privilege. Trusted me to keep quiet and cooperate behind the scenes."

For a second, he didn't think she was going to answer him. Then she squared her shoulders, and locked gazes with him. Suddenly frustrated and angry now, too. "You really want to know?" she bit out eventually.

He slammed his hands on his waist. "Hell, yes, I want to know!"

"I didn't tell you because I wasn't sure you would believe me when I said I had nothing to do with my dad coming here, or contacting me."

He slowly looked her up and down. "So you lied to me, and kept things from me that I needed to know, again!"

She sent him a withering glare. "Can you blame me?"

Yes, as a matter of fact, he could.

She lifted her chin indignantly. Moved close enough to go toe to toe with hin. "You still haven't forgiven me for changing my mind about eloping. Or not telling you of my plans to have a baby on my own before we made love." Her voice took on a low, accusing timbre. "So of course I didn't *want* to tell you any of this! I worried that the mere possibility of my dad reappearing in my life would just be one more thing you'd never be able to forgive me for."

So she hadn't even given him a chance?

She'd just assumed the worst about him and left it that?

"Yet you had no problem confiding in Kyle McCabe," he retorted, incensed.

Adelaide threw up her hands and spun away. "He's a cop. He's able to keep his emotions out of it."

Great. Another low blow. "Unlike me."

Adelaide harrumphed, and pivoted back. "Where I'm concerned, yes!"

Suddenly so much made sense. "That was why McCabe kept stopping by to see you. Why you two chatted so intimately whenever you were together."

Reluctant, she nodded.

Her betrayal stung. Unexpected jealousy roiled in his gut. "Is that where you disappeared yesterday during the festival? To see him?"

Adelaide shoved both hands wearily through her hair. "My father intercepted me when I went out to the parking lot to get the boxes of prizes. So yes, I had to talk to Kyle, let him know that I had 'agreed' to take the babies and run away with my dad. I thought my dad believed me. But I wasn't one hundred percent sure. So I texted Kyle and asked him to meet me at the gas station."

Kyle. Not me. "You could have been followed."

She waved off his concern. "I had an excuse ready, if my dad had turned up there—that we needed to have my SUV ready as backup. And I did need to put gasoline in my vehicle." She released a long, shuddering breath. "But as it turned out, it wasn't necessary because my dad was already off changing his looks again, to a bespectacled, clean-cut, suit-and-tie executive."

Her courage wowed him even as her recklessness made him furious. "You put yourself in danger!"

She disagreed. "My father never would have hurt me."

"He already did."

Adelaide scoffed. "I meant physically."

The thought of something happening to her was enough to make him wild with grief. "You don't know that."

"Yes," she countered just as stubbornly, marching forward, her fists balled at her sides, "I do." Twin spots of color bloomed in her cheeks. "Dad had the chance just now to at least try something, but he didn't. In fact, he wasn't armed at all."

Wyatt blinked. Who *was* she? "You're defending him?"

"I'm saying my part in this is over and hopefully justice will finally be served and I don't want to fight about it." With an exhausted sigh, she sank in a chair.

Wyatt knelt in front of her, so she had no

choice but to look at him. He took her cold, trembling hands in his.

She'd made a mistake. But he would forgive her. On one very important condition. "Promise me this will never happen again," he pressed in a voice as low and urgent as his mood. "You'll never cut me out of the loop." He squeezed her hands. "Tell me that if you had to do it all over again, you would give me a heads-up."

A myriad of emotions came and went in her eyes. Finally she sighed. "I can't do that, because I wouldn't, Wyatt. This was my family's mess to clean up. Not yours. Your family was hurt enough already. No way was I going to let anything else happen. Not to any of you!"

"So you put yourself in harm's way."

"I did what I had to do. I protected your good name. I kept you and the twins and everyone else well away from whatever illegal shenanigans my father was embroiled in. So no one else would have to suffer at his hands. Not ever again."

She was serious, even as she was courageous. Not sure whether he wanted to shake some sense into her or congraulate her, he blurted out, "Damn it, Adelaide…!"

"Damn it, Adelaide, what?" she retorted wearily.

Her stubborn insistence on handling everything by herself was unacceptable. "I can't have you putting yourself and the twins in danger. For any reason!" he warned her quietly.

To his frustration, she stared at him for a long moment, then dug in all the harder. "I can't have you doing that, either, but sometimes life requires us to do the things we do not want to do."

Like stay married to him? he wondered. Even long enough to learn how to co-parent and consciously uncouple?

All he knew for certain was that the woman who had made love with him so tenderly, the wife who had finally started to open up her heart and soul to him, was nowhere to be found.

"You really will not admit you're in the wrong

here?" he said slowly. "For lying to me, and keeping me in the dark? For not giving me the chance to be the husband I should be, the husband that you have every right to want and need?"

Still holding his gaze, she disengaged their hands and shook her head. Letting him know in that one instant that she was always going to shut him out. And never more routinely than when it really counted.

He stood, aware he'd never felt more betrayed and more bitterly disillusioned in his life.

He couldn't live like that.

Neither could she.

Their kids really couldn't.

"Then the two of us having nothing else to say."

Chapter Fifteen

"Wyatt *left* you?" Chance asked later the same day, shooting her an incredulous look.

Adelaide nodded miserably. The news of her father's arrest and the drama that had ensued preceding it had spread through the town like wildfire. By noon, it was on the news reports all over the state. Knowing it would be even more of a story if the press learned she and Wyatt had also split up over it, Adelaide was doing her best to keep the dissolution of their relationship within the Lockhart family.

Hence, she had asked Sage and Lucille to come out to Wind River to babysit the twins while she worked on finding them a place other than the ranch to live. Starting immediately.

"He got dressed and walked out midargument. I thought—hoped—he might simmer down and come back," she admitted with a weary shake of her head. *Say he was sorry. That he still wanted to be with me.* "But instead, he texted me that I could stay at the ranch as long I wanted." She drew in an unsteady breath, achingly aware just what an unacceptable idea that was, with her feeling the way she did about him.

She turned away from their sympathetic looks, swallowing hard. "Or until my place is finished. That we could alternate care of the twins with your family's help." Hot angry tears pricked her eyes. "I assume to prevent us from running into each other."

Molly moved closer, aghast. "Was all this before or after he gave you your Valentine's Day gift?"

"We never got around to that. I mean, he tried last night, when we got home from the festival, but I couldn't let him do something sweet for me when I was about to betray him."

Molly and Chance exchanged troubled looks.

"So you knew how he would likely take your secrecy?" Chance asked.

"I didn't have a choice."

Chance gave her a look that said of course she had. She could have trusted his brother to keep quiet and cooperate with law enforcement, too.

Except Wyatt would have wanted to defend her. Or go in her stead. And if her father had seen Wyatt, he would have been tipped off and bolted.

The situation would have been more complicated and precarious than ever.

Wearily, Adelaide turned her attention back to the partially framed construction of the addition to her house. "Anyway, the reason I called you both over here was to ask you if it would be possible to put an immediate hold on construction, so I could move back in with the twins."

"Sure, we can put a halt to the project," Chance said. "Happens all the time. But with the foundation poured, and some of the framing started, you may want to go a little while longer...at least get the shell up, roof on. Doors and windows on."

It would certainly look a lot better. "How long will that take?" Adelaide asked.

Molly and Chance considered. "A few weeks, if we rush," Molly said.

Only one problem. "The twins and I don't have any place to stay."

"There's always the bunkhouse," Chance pointed out kindly. "You were going to stay there before..."

...*everything blew up*, Adelaide finished silently. *Before Wyatt and I discovered we had twins, and I fell for him all over again.*

"Lucille's offered." To Adelaide's relief, her

mother-in-law had been very kind about every-thing, in fact, when they'd spoken.

"But?" Chance prompted.

Guilt and misery roiled inside her. "I don't want Wyatt not to be able to see his mom when-ever he wants. If I'm at the Circle H, I would interfere with their ability to see each other un-encumbered. Which would in turn interfere with their making up over the whole keeping his learning disabilities a secret from everyone quarrel."

Molly squinted. "I have a feeling there's some-thing more…"

Adelaide sighed. "She also told me I'm making a huge mistake, allowing her son to walk out on me. And that I should use every tool at my dis-posal—including bunking with her—to bring him back home." Especially since that proposed "arrangement" was what had brought them all together in the first place.

"Maybe Lucille is right," Molly said gently. "It

is a little early to be giving up on everything you and Wyatt shared the past few weeks."

If only it were that easy, she thought in frustration. "He gave up on us first. Besides, what am I supposed to do? Beg him to stay? He's clearly never forgiven me for changing my mind about eloping, or not telling him of my plans to have a family alone before we finally made love. In his mind, this is just one more thing he'll never be able to forget."

And she couldn't bear failing. Not again. Not when there was even more at stake.

A commiserating silence fell.

Eventually, Chance asked, "Does this mean you're going to consciously uncouple after all and go ahead with the divorce?"

Adelaide released a weary breath, aware she was just going to have to find a way to overcome a broken heart. Again. "It's not as if we were ever really together." They'd been playing house while they embarked on a wildly passionate and reckless love affair. "We were just doing what we thought needed to be done for the kids at the time." The honeymoon atmosphere they had enjoyed had been because of their babies, their growing love for them.

Brows rose.

Adelaide went to her fridge and looked inside to see what was there.

Not much, unless one counted condiments.

Making a mental note that she was going to have to go grocery shopping before she picked up the twins, she swung back around. "The good news is Jenny and Jake are too young to realize what their dad and I could have had, if only we were compatible. Which we are definitely not."

"Right now you're not," Chance agreed flatly.

As if it were all her fault!

Ignoring her mounting pain and indignation, Adelaide shrugged and looked her soon to be ex-in-laws in the eye. "Look, I wish Wyatt and I could have the kind of forever and ever relationship that the two of you have, but we don't. The bottom line is my dad was right. Wyatt is always going to be ready to walk out the door at the first disappointment, and I can't live with someone who is never going to be able to find it in his heart to forgive me for my past, present or future transgressions. So, it's better for everyone we cut our losses and part now."

Molly reached out and took Chance's hand. The couple was the picture of loving solidarity.

"We would agree if we thought it was my brother's forgiveness that you really wanted, Molly," Chance said quietly.

Eyes solemn, Molly added, "But we don't."

WYATT RETURNED TO his ranch house as soon as he got the text from his mother. "Adelaide left?"

Lucille pulled a small load of baby clothes out of the dryer and carried the basket to the sofa. "She had to go into town to give the sheriff's department her statement. And she wanted to check on the possibility of halting construction and moving back into her home."

Wyatt looked at the twins, who were sleeping in their Pack 'N Plays, and Sage, who was in his kitchen doing what she always did when under stress—baking.

He returned to his mother's side.

He didn't want to talk about any of this, but he knew his mother wasn't going to let it go until they did. "So she told you?"

Lucille folded a blue onesie. "And of course I think it's my fault."

"What? Why?" Wyatt went to the fridge to get a bottle of water.

"The mistakes I made when you were growing up."

Not the three Ds again. He uncapped the bottle. "Mom. It's over."

"I don't think so." Lucille watched him take a long thirsty drink. "Otherwise, you wouldn't still be reliving it. Or worried Adelaide isn't strong enough to stick with you through thick and thin."

The knowledge that his wife had betrayed him—again—had filled him with a numbness that refused to go away. "Believe me, she's plenty strong enough," he groused. "Otherwise…"

His mother put a folded pink onesie next to the blue. "Not compassionate enough to help you deal with whatever lingering feelings you have about your learning disabilities?"

Wondering how long it was going to take him to recover this time, Wyatt paced. "I put those behind me years ago."

"You can't forgive her for what her dad did, then?"

Oh, for…! Wyatt swung back around. "I can't forgive her for what *she* did. Not telling me that Paul was back in her life, trying to drag her into his mess. Or, swearing afterward, that if the same thing happened all over again, she wouldn't change a thing."

Lucille put little white undershirts in a separate stack. "She's not allowed to have a different opinion than you?"

Wyatt scowled. "She's not allowed to *not trust me*, Mom."

"Did she say that?"

Of course she hadn't! Wyatt tossed his empty

bottle into the recycling bin. "Adelaide's actions demonstrate it time and again! We elope. She leaves. We take a leap of faith ten years later and finally hook up. She changes her mind about turning that into something more, too. Then we find out her kids are mine, too, and decide to make the best of a difficult situation and raise our babies together. And what does she do? The one thing that will drive me around the bend! She puts herself and our kids in danger!"

"First of all, Wyatt, your children were safe in the ranch house with you. Only she went out to meet Paul. Second of all, I think she viewed it as putting herself on the line in order to keep not just you but the entire Lockhart clan out of jeopardy." She slanted him a pointed look. "And it's my understanding that the sheriff's department had been surveilling her with her complete cooperation since last summer. They knew where Adelaide was, and who she was with, at all times. And she did that *not only for our fam-*

ily, but because she saw it as the best way to protect you and your kids."

"Sounds to me like a woman in love!" Sage said from the kitchen. "And if you don't want to believe that, you should see some of the photos that just hit the internet news sites on this breaking story."

She strode over with her tablet, x-ing out the screen that held the recipe she had been following. "Marco Maletti hit the jackpot with these."

Too late, Wyatt recalled that the photographer had been hired by Hope to keep taking photos during the Laramie Chili Festival to feed to the press. There were pictures of him and Adelaide together, early in the morning, before she'd seen her dad, looking happy and completely wrapped up with each other. More with them both working the festival, in the go-fishing-game booth and the cutting-horse demonstration. Photos of him, with the twins in the kangaroo carrier, taking in the sights. And shots of Adelaide being unexpectedly waylaid in the parking lot of the fairgrounds. Her expression stricken, then happy. Heartbroken. Tense. Worried. Sober. And, as she finally walked away from Paul Smythe, completely devastated.

Clearly she'd been through hell yesterday.

And what had he done?

Added to her misery.

He swore quietly.

"I can see you think you failed Adelaide," Lucille said gently.

Why sugarcoat the situation? Aware this was just another "test" he had bombed, Wyatt shook his head. "I did." And his screwup had nothing to do with his learning disabilities. It had to do with his heart.

No wonder Adelaide had run from him.

What was amazing was that she had ever stayed.

"You can still fix this," his mother said quietly.

Could he?

The larger question—was it fair of him to even try?

All this time he had thought it was Adelaide's issues keeping them apart. Now he saw it was his.

His cynicism.

His refusal to trust.

Never mind his unwillingness to understand, empathize…and forgive.

Shoulders slumping, he sat on the sofa and buried his head in his hands.

His mother put a comforting hand on his shoulder. "The point is we all make mistakes, son. You bungled it with Adelaide. Your father and I messed up with you. At the time, of course, your father and I both thought we were doing what was right for you, covering up the dyslexia, dysgraphia and dyscalculia. Shadowing you to make sure you didn't make any public mistakes that would have caused you further embarrassment. But now I wonder if maybe he and I were covering up our own inadequacies, rather than what we perceived as your deficiencies."

Aware he wasn't the only one recently who

had been driven to do some soul-searching, Wyatt listened.

"You see, your dad and I had to really struggle to leave our meager beginnings behind and achieve social and financial success. We didn't want any of you children to have to fight that hard," Lucille continued pensively.

"You wanted to protect us, and do everything you could for us because we were your kids. I get that, Mom. Now more than ever because of the twins."

She nodded, accepting the partial reprieve. "But back then, I worried too much about what other people thought about us," she admitted, voice quavering. "And not enough about what I felt and knew to be true deep in my heart, which is that academic success is only a small part of a person's worth." She paused to look into his eyes. "Courage and grit and determination and kindness and compassion are worth a whole hell of a lot more."

A surge of emotion rose within him. "I'm glad you feel that way," Wyatt said gruffly.

Tears blurred his mother's eyes.

The affection she felt for him deepened her voice. "I loved you all equally. And I still do." She hugged him fiercely, then drew back to look into his face. Even more sober now. "And if I failed to communicate that, if you feel I some-how loved you less or was any less proud of you—" her voice broke and tears flowed freely down her cheeks "—then I apologize to you with every fiber of my being." She grasped his shoulders, making sure she had his full atten-tion.

With an unsteady breath, she said, "Don't make my mistake, Wyatt. Don't let fear of being hurt drive your actions." She paused to look into his eyes. "And most important of all, don't fail to communicate what you really feel, deep in your heart."

THANKS TO THE offer from Lucille and Sage to babysit the twins while he cleared his head and figured out the best way to remedy the mess he and Adelaide were in, Wyatt spent the next several hours working with his horses. Decision made, he returned to the Wind River ranch house. And discovered the first glitch in his plan.

He stared at his mom. "Adelaide wants me to meet her in town?" He'd thought she was coming back to the ranch after her errands.

Lucille looked at his disheveled state. "At her home."

Aware he hadn't had time to shave and shower yet—and he needed to do both before seeing his wife—he shrugged out of his jacket. Okay, this wasn't necessarily a bad sign, he told himself. "Am I supposed to bring the twins?"

"No. But don't worry. Sage and I can continue to babysit this evening."

"Anything to help you set things right," Sage said, starry-eyed as ever, looking as emotional as he felt.

Wyatt felt a catch in his throat. What did his suddenly deeply concerned mother and sister know that he didn't? "Did she say why she wants me there?"

Reluctantly, Lucille admitted, "She wants to talk about how things are going to work with you-all going forward. She thought it would be better to get that ironed out sooner rather than later."

Damn.

He'd thought—hoped—he would have a little more time before Adelaide went into full dissolution mode and made their relationship officially a thing of the past.

Apparently not.

Which meant he was going to have to do what he loathed most. Admit he was in over his head and ask for help.

He looked at his mother and sister. Aware they had always stood nearby, ready to assist.

Resolved to prove his learning deficiencies didn't make him any less capable than the rest of his sibs, he'd rarely let them.

It looked like that, too, was about to change.

ADELAIDE WALKED BACK and forth, a bundle of nerves.

Where was he?

Had Wyatt changed his mind about meeting with her tonight?

What could be keeping him?

A peek outside showed a cold rain beginning to fall.

It wasn't supposed to last long.

But it added an aura of gloom to the already risky evening.

What if she'd made a mistake? Like Wyatt, assumed too much? What if he didn't want what she wanted after all?

Headlights swept the front of her house. An engine cut. A door opened, then finally slammed. Footsteps moved across her porch and moments later the doorbell rang.

Heart in her throat, tears pricking behind her eyes, Adelaide smoothed her skirt and headed for the door. Jerking in a breath, she swung it open.

Wyatt stood on her porch. In tweed sport coat, pale blue shirt, pressed jeans, and boots, a black Resistol slanted low across his brow, he looked both solemn and hopeful. And ruggedly handsome as all get-out.

His gaze took in her upswept hair, figure-hugging red knit dress, and heels. She'd worried the care she had taken getting ready might be too much. Apparently it wasn't.

"You look…amazing…" he said huskily, gazing at her in a way no one ever had before, with breath-stealing tenderness.

A surge of warmth went through her as her eyes tracked his. "So do you."

He handed her a bouquet of red roses and a heart-shaped satin box of chocolate candy. "These are for you." His rough-hewn voice was tinged with apology and another more sober emotion she couldn't identify. "A belated Valentine's Day."

Regret poured through her as she thought about how she had pushed him away the evening before, when he'd been trying to celebrate their anniversary. "Thank you." Adelaide swallowed around the sudden dryness of her throat. "I have something for you, too." Opening the door wider, she ushered him inside. She'd lit a fire in the hearth and set the table for two. A big envelope sat on the entry table. She handed it to him, her heart thudding uncertainly in her chest. "This came for us this afternoon."

It had seemed like a sign. She hoped he would consider it one, too. She set the flowers and candy on the entry table while he removed the papers inside. His eyes filled just the way hers had when he laid eyes on the document. "The twins' official birth certificates."

"You're now legally their dad."

A flicker of happiness crossed his face before his expression grew solemn once again. "Thank you for showing this to me."

Deliberately, she kept her eyes locked with his. "Thank you for impregnating me."

He chuckled. "Adelaide…"

She lifted a palm. Now that the mood had lightened slightly, she was determined to get this out before either of them screwed up any more. Taking a deep breath, she began, "We've never really talked about what went wrong after our night in Aspen. And we need to, Wyatt."

He looked wary again. "I'm listening."

She moved closer. "I always regretted not giving us a chance to see if things could have worked when we eloped. So when we met up again in Aspen that night and the sparks lit, I decided to just go with it. And make love. I knew I should have told you that I already had plans to have a baby, and indeed was convinced I was already pregnant. But I didn't think you'd understand, and I didn't want to miss the chance to be with you."

Adelaide watched the regret come into his eyes and rushed on, "I just figured it was a one-night stand. A kind of 'what if' for us. But when you seemed to want more than that, I got even more scared. It hurt so much when we split up the first time, I didn't think I could bear to go through that again, so…" Pain lancing her heart, she continued, "I left you first."

"And I let you."

"That was the right thing to do then." She sucked in a breath, determined to own up to every one of the many mistakes she had made, then suffer the fallout. "I was still in victim mode, still blaming you for everything that had gone wrong between us. Still telling myself that you and I would never have anything long-term because *you* were never going to be able to forgive *me* for my past, present and future mistakes. But I've realized something, Wyatt." Her lower lip trembled as she revealed her biggest vulnerability of all. "It's never been you I needed forgiveness from," she whispered. "It's myself. I'm the one who wouldn't let the past go. Even when I saw you were willing to. I'm the one who couldn't trust.

"But I can't do that anymore, Wyatt. I can't punish myself with fear, or keep the barriers up around my heart. I'm going to accept the mistakes I've made, and there have been a lot, and forgive myself, because only then will I be able to go on and make things right."

Leaning toward her, Wyatt gathered her in his arms and held her close. As she gazed up at him, she saw something she hadn't expected—understanding.

"You're not the only one who's done some soul-searching." He stroked his thumb across her cheek. Eyes darkening, he confessed, "I was angry when I found out your father had been back in touch and you hadn't told me. But it wasn't really your participation in the law-enforcement sting that upset me. Or what your father had done."

She gripped the solid warmth of his biceps, listening intently.

"I've been ticked off because you turned away from me twice when I thought we had it all. In Vegas, and then again in Aspen. This whole time, I've been afraid to let us get too close because I was scared if I did that you'd leave me again."

How well she understood that.

"So this time," his said, lips thinning ruefully, "I took a page from your playbook, and when I found out you'd been shutting me out, I turned away first. Not because I couldn't forgive you for everything that had happened in the past, because in truth I had done that long ago. I just wouldn't admit it. Not to you, not to anyone."

Adelaide understood that, too.

They'd both feared being vulnerable.

It had been easier to simply stay at war with each other.

He searched her face. "And it wasn't because I didn't understand the situation you were in. Or accept that you were doing what you should have done—cooperate with law enforcement and follow their directions to the max. It was because I was scared, now that things had gotten complicated again, that you were going to walk out on me. Again."

"I'm not going to do that, Wyatt. *Ever*. I'm going to do what all those long-married couples do, and trust that I love you now as much as I always have, and always will, and show up every day with the kind of love and trust and commitment you and I should have had all along."

"Darlin'." His tone left no doubt about what he wanted. He lifted her face to his. Slanting his lips over hers, he kissed her tenderly until she kissed him back just as sweetly. "I love you, too. And I'm as all in now as you are," he promised gruffly.

He grinned at the tears of happiness slipping down her face, then gently brushed them away. "I want us to have that forever and ever we—and our kids—deserve. Which is why I'm going to do what I was planning to do last night. And—" he got down on one knee, removed a box from his pocket "—propose." His voice caught, moisture suddenly glittering in his eyes, matching hers.

"Marry me, Adelaide," he urged huskily. "This time, for all the right reasons."

A sob catching in her throat, Adelaide pulled him to his feet and took him joyfully into her arms. "Yes, Wyatt. I will!"

Epilogue

Two weeks later

"Your mother wasn't kidding when she said she was going to spare no expense with her Welcome to the Family party for us," Adelaide said as Wyatt turned their pickup truck into the lane that led to the Circle H Ranch.

Several hundred vehicles lined both sides of the long tree-lined drive. Cowboys were doubling as valets. On the grounds between the newly renovated ranch house and bunkhouse, a dance floor and bandstand had been put up.

Tables and chairs were quickly filling with the denim-clad guests.

Wyatt parked in the spot close to the house that had been reserved for them.

"How do you think Lucille's going to take our news?" Adelaide asked as they removed the twins from their safety seats.

"What news?" Lucille asked, hurrying to join them. "And what are you two doing in evening wear? I told you this party was Western casual!"

Wyatt and Adelaide exchanged cheeky grins, aware they would both be changing later. "Do you want to tell her or shall I?" she asked.

He figured, given the hell he had put his mother through over the years, this news was his to deliver. "We're getting married, Mom."

"You *are* married!" Lucille huffed. "For ten years now!"

"Yes, but you didn't get to see it, and back then, we didn't really mean it. Not the way we do now. So…"

For the first time he could recall, his mother was completely speechless.

Tears glittered in her eyes.

She opened her mouth, tried to speak but no sound came out.

Pressing her hand to her suddenly quivering lips, Lucille hugged them both.

Recovering, she whacked Wyatt lightly on the shoulder. "You should have told me. And you're ruining my makeup."

He was beginning to get a little choked up himself. "Isn't that what weddings are for? Happy tears?" he joked.

Lucille cried all the harder.

Waving off the emotion, she stepped back to admire them both. Adelaide wore a knee-length ivory sheath with a high collared beaded jacket that made the most of her feminine curves. Wyatt was in a dark gray suit and tie.

"You look gorgeous," Lucille said, gathering her wits about her. "But we have to get everything organized."

"Relax, Mom." Wyatt nodded behind him.

His siblings were all doing their part. Directing everyone to pitch in and move the white folding chairs to the grassy expanse on the other side of the bandstand. A rose-covered arbor, originally meant as a party-picture-taking backdrop, was serving as their altar. Reverend Bleeker, from the community chapel in town, was speaking to Molly and Chance who'd been tapped to serve as their maid of honor and best man.

"So everyone knows?" Lucille asked.

"Just the sibs. The guests are as surprised as you. Speaking of which…" Wyatt nodded at the familiar man in uniform walking toward them.

"Zane!" Lucille cried all the harder at the sight of her youngest, rarely home son. "He's here, too?"

Zane reached them. He had recovered from the relatively minor mission-related injuries that had plagued him at Christmas, and had gone out on another assignment with his unit. But he was now Stateside again, at least briefly, to his entire family's delight.

"My most hardheaded, hard-hearted brother finally getting hitched to the woman of his dreams? I couldn't miss that!" He hugged them all as the band began to play.

"That's our cue."

Lucille took Jenny; Zane carried little Jake.

Sage appeared with a bouquet of flowers, and a lapel pin for Wyatt, Nick Monroe by her side, looking surprisingly protective and possessive.

Wyatt took Adelaide's hand. His family took their seats. Together, they made their way to the satin runner that had been laid out. Paused.

So much had happened over the past month he could hardly believe it, but looking down into his bride's radiant face, he knew it was true. He and Adelaide had put all the heartache of the past to rest and formed the family they had always wanted.

He had promised to become more active in the family charitable foundation. She would assist him in the training of cutting horses. In both activities, as well as with their parenting, they intended to further the bonds between them and work side by side.

Paul Smythe had been apprehended. The former CFO had pleaded guilty to all charges, and received a reduced sentence to a white-collar prison for returning all remaining cash to the Lockhart Foundation. Adelaide was still pretty hurt, but Wyatt was encouraging her to forgive her father and find a way to forge some sort of relationship. After all, Paul was the twins' grandfather, and the only dad she had. Yes, mistakes had been made. But a new path could always be forged.

Best of all, he and the love of his life were finally together and would be from this day forward. As friends and lovers, co-parents and soul mates, husband and wife, and all-around damn good time.

He took her other hand and turned her to face him. Gazing deep into her eyes, he said softly,

"I love you with all my heart, Addie. You know that."

She shimmered with joy. "I do. And I love you, too, Wyatt. So very much."

Happiness floated between them, as endless as the deep blue Texas sky above.

The final strains of Rascal Flatts' "Bless the Broken Road" ended. Wyatt looked at the woman who had always meant so much to him. The life partner who had lovingly showed him just how meaningful and satisfying their life could be. He squeezed her hand. "Ready?"

The love she felt for him in her eyes, Adelaide rose on tiptoe and kissed him tenderly. "You better believe I'm ready, cowboy," she told him joyously.

He grinned and offered her his arm. The strains of the deeply sentimental "Valentine" filled the sweet, flower-scented Texas air. And the wedding they had waited their whole life for began.

* * * * *